SAM CRESCENT

EVERNIGHT PUBLISHING ®

www.evernightpublishing.com

MINE

Copyright© 2017

Sam Crescent

Editor: Karyn White

Cover Artist: Sour Cherry Designs

Jacket Design: Jay Aheer

ISBN: 978-1-77339-205-9

ALL RIGHTS RESERVED

SAM CRESCENT

DEDICATION

I want to thank all of my wonderful readers for their amazing love and support. Also, to my lovely editor Karyn for her patience with me, and of course to Evernight, for giving the Trojans a home. Love you all.

SAM CRESCENT

MINE

Trojans MC, 5

Sam Crescent

Copyright © 2016

Prologue

Five years ago

"What the fuck is your problem?" Daisy asked, staring at his girlfriend. She wasn't his old lady as she didn't come by the club, nor did he want to claim her in front of his brothers. To be honest, there wasn't anything he actually liked about her other than the fact she was a regular fuck away from the club.

"You pick out my clothes, and you go through my phone. You're not letting me breathe, and you expect me to be okay with that?"

Daisy had known he wasn't like many of the guys he hung around with. His brothers at the club were happy to live apart from their woman, but he'd always been wired a different way. He liked picking out his woman's clothing, and finding out how she spent her day, and even giving instructions for how he wanted certain things.

Being the man in the family, the dominant, turned him the fuck on. He wasn't a cruel man, and when he thought about life if he was to ever get married, having a woman accept those needs inside him was paramount.

"You're controlling, Daisy. We're not even fucking exclusive, and you're demanding shit."

"Laura, this is who I am. I told you I liked shit done a certain way—"

"What you want is archaic, and I don't want that. I want to pick out my own clothing, and have a life away from you. Women stopped being doormats fucking years ago. We don't need to be trapped in marriage, or kept at home."

He'd treasure any woman he put his ring on her finger. Not only would his real woman get his ring, she'd get his cut, and he'd claim her in front of his brothers. Laura was not the kind of woman that he wanted.

"This is who I am."

"Then go ahead and find a woman dumb enough to give you what you want. It's archaic, and fucked up. You're a great fuck, Daisy, but it's not what I want, and I doubt *any* woman is going to want that."

He watched as Laura stormed out of his room, and his door slammed.

"Wow, talk about fucked up," Knuckles said coming into the room.

"What the fuck are you still doing here?"

"So, you're the master of the house?" Knuckles looked around the room.

"What?" Daisy ran a hand down his face, trying to clear the fog that had settled over his brain. He wasn't in the best of moods right now. Laura had shouted out their shit for one of his brothers to hear, and now he was pissed, really pissed.

"You know, the master of your castle, the one in control. In a way you're like a 1950s man or a dominant. It's interesting."

"I don't have a fucking clue what you're talking about."

"Of course you don't." Knuckles gave him a pointed look. "It's not wrong, you know, or sick."

"According to Laura, I'm fucked up." Daisy had been hearing more and more of Laura's complaints, and thinking back over his life with her, he couldn't even remember why he'd tried to make something more out of their relationship.

"It's not fucked up. I've heard of men liking that."

"You're trying to make me feel better?" Daisy asked.

"No. I'm speaking the truth. We can't help what we like. I'd say you were fucked up if you got off on beating women to death, and that got your nut off. You don't. You like to control, to be in charge. I get it."

"Are you like me?" Daisy asked.

Knuckles smirked. "Think more of the chains, whips, Domination, and slaves, and you're more on track."

"I don't need whips or chains to keep me satisfied."

"That's where we differ. You'll find a woman for you, and I'll find a woman for me. Until then, we're good to fuck all the free pussy at the club."

Daisy never took another woman again, and used the pussy at the club to get his rocks off.

Chapter One

Present day

"What the fuck are you talking about?" Duke asked, glaring across the desk at him. Daisy had been thinking about this for the past week, ever since he'd spoken to Maria. He'd kept her at arm's length, and not even taken the time to talk to her about anything. All he'd done was ignore her, being a complete and total bastard to her, fucking other women even though it was her face he saw every single night.

She'd taken him by surprise, pretty much daring him to take her. Fuck, her words about being wanted, being consumed, and even a little dominated. Okay, it wasn't chains, whips, and leather pants with her calling him "Master", but it was another kind of domination. She wanted him to be the boss of her, to love, and to guide her.

He'd not been able to resist testing her just a little bit. This past week, to see if she would follow what he wanted, he had entered her room early in the morning, and gone through her wardrobe, picking out her clothing. Daisy had also told her that she was only to wear what he'd put out. There was no way he could survive watching her without a bra with her large tits bouncing freely. He'd made her wear a bra, a sundress, with no panties. When she'd been leaning over the pool table on that first day, he'd run his hand up the inside of her dress to see if she'd followed that simple instruction. She had. She'd been bare to the touch, and so fucking perfect, she'd made his cock ache.

Maria hadn't fought him, and now it was time for him to face the reality of what he wanted. She'd given him a chance, and he wasn't going to let her down.

"I need to take Maria away for the next few weeks, maybe even a month. I don't know how long I'm going to be."

"Where the fuck is this coming from?" Duke asked.

"Look, I've been given an opportunity, and I can't turn it down, nor can I run from it."

"That's fucking vague."

"When you had a chance to make Holly your woman, you took it, no questions asked. I've got a chance to make Maria my old lady, and I can't lose that chance. I've got this one shot, and if I fuck it up, there's not going to be anyone else in the world for me."

Duke leaned back, and stared at him. "Maria? Your sister's best friend."

"Yes."

"What's happening with Beth?"

"I'm hoping she'll be protected at the club while I'm away. I'll go and talk to her. I'll do whatever you need me to do." Daisy gripped the back of the chair. "I want you to keep an eye on Knuckles. I don't want him near my sister."

"So now I've got to be a babysitter, and keep one of my boys away from your girl?" Duke asked. "I've got work to do. I'm not just sitting around on my ass."

"We've got no drug runs planned for the next month. You don't need me directly, and you can still get in touch with me." Daisy tapped the back of the chair. "This is something I need to do." He thought about Laura and couldn't help but worry that if he took this next step with Maria, he wasn't going to come back from it. Holy shit, he was starting to sound like a pussy. He didn't question his need for what he wanted. Maria had come to him, and he was going to test her, and see how far she could go.

Duke sighed. "Fine. I'll keep an eye on Knuckles, but I'm not going to separate your sister from him if she doesn't want it. Give him a warning or something, but don't start a fight. I won't have any shit like that."

"What are you going to do when Matthew wants to join the club?" Daisy asked.

Matthew was Duke's son from a previous marriage before he married and claimed Holly as his own. They both now had a son together, Drake. It sounded more complicated than it actually was.

"He's nearly seventeen," Duke said.

"I remember the kind of shit I was getting into at that age."

Duke stood up moving toward the window to overlook the back of the clubhouse. Daisy knew what he'd find. Holly with Drake, and her best friend Mary with her kid, Pike's daughter, Starlight.

"He's having sex," Duke said.

"Damn, he's like his father."

"I fucking caught him in the back of my truck. He was near the clubhouse, and I was heading home when Holly sent me a text that Matthew wasn't home. I tell you, it's not a pretty sight seeing your son screwing some girl. I made him deep clean the truck before I let Holly back inside."

Daisy burst out laughing. "Bet you never imagined having to be a cock blocker."

"When he's eighteen he wants to start prospecting for the club. Holly wants him to take some time, and think about his future."

"What do you want for him?"

"I want him to be sure of what he wants. He's my son, my oldest son, and I love him. The club life, it's hard, intense, and it's fucking dangerous. We live with that danger every single day. We've set ourselves a comfortable life here, but it doesn't mean shit can't go bad. Look at The Skulls and Chaos Bleeds, not to mention the clubs out there that have been wiped out. I know we're not immortal." Duke stepped, looking away from his woman outside of the window. "I never thought I'd have to deal with this shit yet."

"Boys grow into men. Matthew, he's a great guy."

"You think I should let him join?"

Daisy shrugged. "I don't have a son. I know what I wanted to do at his age. I wanted pussy, no rules, and I wanted to be part of the club. He's a boy racing toward being a man, but he's not a man yet. It takes a lot of shit to happen to make you a man. If he's anything like you, he's not going to have any problem."

"Thanks, Daisy, I appreciate that."

"You're a good Prez. We'll put Matthew through his paces if he decides to take to the club life. You never know, it might be what he's missing to give him that edge."

"Until then I've talked with him about bagging his shit up. The last thing I need is for him to come home with a girl his own age or older, pregnant. Fucking nightmare just thinking about it."

Daisy chuckled. "I'll be heading out tomorrow."

"Wow, you're not going to give her much time to back out."

"I've got one chance. I'm going to take it."

"If you need us, give us a call."

Nodding his head, Daisy made his way out of the clubhouse, and paused when he saw Knuckles at the bar reading. He couldn't recall a time when he'd seen a book in Knuckles's hand. It was a strange sight, and he pulled his cell phone out and took a quick snap. "Got to keep this for the scrapbooks."

"Fuck off, Daisy."

"Where did you get it?" Daisy asked.

"Your sister."

Gritting his teeth, he took a seat even though he wanted to smash his fist against the bastard's smug face.

"It's nice to know that you'll shut the fuck up," Knuckles said.

"I want you to stay away from Beth."

"I'm not bothering her. I'm sitting here reading."

"I'm about to head out with Maria, and take a chance at something. Beth is, I don't know, she's got something going on, and I don't know what it is. Either way, I don't want you anywhere near her."

Knuckles chuckled. "This is more than being the big brother, right?"

"Yes. I know what your deal is. I don't want that near Beth."

"You ever thought that your sister needs *that*?"

"I will kill you if you lay a finger on my sister, Knuckles. I'm not joking around about that."

"I get it. Keep my hands to myself. I'll do that, but if she needs something, Daisy, I'm not going to turn her down. She's hurting, but she's not broken. I will not do anything that could risk her overall wellbeing." Knuckles held his hands up in surrender. "That's the best I can offer you, brother."

Daisy was torn between staying and going. He wanted this chance with Maria, damn it.

"I remember what we talked about a few years back, Daisy. Beth's old enough to make her own choices, and you've got no choice but to trust her, and to trust me."

"It's you I don't trust. Where is my sister?"

"She came out for some food, and went back to Maria's room. That girl is pissed at you."

"Beth?"

"No, Maria. She wouldn't even look at you yesterday, and Beth's been giving you the stink eye. You've messed up, bro."

He'd heard enough. It was time for him to go hunting for what he really wanted.

****

"What's going on with you and my brother?" Beth asked, walking in the bedroom behind her.

They had just finished breakfast, and Maria wasn't interested in talking about Daisy, or what was going on between them. She had opened herself up, and he'd humiliated her. He hadn't taken her seriously at all, and that just pissed her off.

"Nothing."

"I know you've got a serious crush on him, but this past week you've done everything to avoid him." Beth reached out, touching her arm. "You can talk to me."

"When are you going to tell him what happened?"

Beth froze up. "Never."

"They deserve to pay for what they did to you."

"It was only one—"

"I don't care, Beth. He doesn't deserve to be walking around free while you're fighting." She loved her friend dearly. If she hadn't come with Beth this summer, she'd have spent it trying to find a way to hurt the man who'd hurt her friend.

"Look, he's untouchable. This is not about me. I'll be fine, more than fine. I've even been thinking of going to the college near Vale Valley rather than back home. It will be fun."

"You're not wanting to return home?"

"The more I'm here, Maria, the more I feel I'm at home. The Trojans are part of my brother, and they never make me feel uncomfortable."

"What about Knuckles?" Maria had seen that brother staring at Beth. It was so damn obvious to anyone who watched that he clearly had a thing for her. Did Beth see it?

"He's nice, and he likes to talk."

"I doubt that's all he likes."

"I'm not looking for anything. Knuckles is a nice guy. He's not dangerous."

Maria chuckled. "I used to think I was the innocent one out of the two of us."

"What do you mean?"

"All of the men in the club are dangerous, and you think a guy named Knuckles, isn't? They're road names, right? Knuckles isn't his real name, but I can take a guess to how he got it."

Beth shook her head. "I don't want to talk about it. I'd rather talk about you and my brother."

"Of course you would. Nothing is going on between me and your brother."

Someone knocked on her door, and Maria shouted that it was open. Daisy was the one to open the door.

"I want a word with Beth," he said.

Even though he pissed her off and upset her, Maria still grew wet at the sight of him. He wasn't a small man. Daisy was large, scary, muscular, and covered in ink. The biggest of tats was the daisy on his back, which he'd gotten when he was drunk.

"Go," Maria said.

Beth gave her hand a squeeze, and left her alone. They left her room, and Maria didn't want to be locked up in it. Grabbing some sneakers from the corner, she quickly pulled them on, and moved out of her room. She made sure she was quiet as she closed her door, and walked toward the main part of the club.

"Sneaking around?" Landon asked.

He was coming up behind her from the toilet. During the summer she had learned that he'd been a prospect for the club until recently. The brothers had finally voted him in to be a fully patched in member of the MC.

"Not sneaking."

"I don't know. Tiptoeing around a clubhouse isn't a good thing for anyone, man or woman."

"I'm heading outside for some fresh air. I need to think."

"Lead the way. I'm waiting for Zoe to finish up with Raoul so we can head back to our dorm. It's our last semester, and then I'm going to be hanging around full time."

"You're not going to work anywhere else? Maybe go for some internships in business?"

"Nah, I'm not interested in wearing a suit or shit. Duke's going to let me handle some of the books, and that's all I need in my life." Landon laughed. "I'll never be the kind of guy who can handle a suit."

Maria hadn't found suits on men all that attractive. Daisy had always been different. Whenever she saw him over the years, he'd capture her attention, and nothing could pull her away. She liked his don't care attitude, along with the fact he was hot. Maria hadn't been hot, growing up. She'd been the chunky kid. She and Beth both had.

Now, she was still fuller, and she loved her food. Since being around Holly and Mary, it had only increased her love of food. Those two women were deadly for a woman's hips, and she should know. She'd gone up a dress size in the weeks she'd been at the clubhouse, and she'd visited the women at their homes. Deadly, the pair of them.

"Hey, Landon. Hey, Maria. You two okay?" Holly asked. She had Drake in a baby swing and was gently moving it to the squealing boy.

"Good, I'm good. What about you?" Maria asked.

"Me, I was telling hot little Maria that I'm not cut out for a suit. My sexy body needs more focus than being confined to something tight and restricting."

Mary snorted. "Seriously, you're the most conceited man I know, and I'm married to Pike. He's pretty conceited, too."

"We're good in bed," Landon said.

"Stop giving my wife ideas," Pike said, coming up behind Mary. He wrapped his arm around her, kissing her neck.

Maria loved the club, and she understood why Daisy was part of it. If he'd given her a chance after she exposed her innermost wants, she'd never have made him pick between her and the club. She wanted to be with him *and* the club.

Everyone started talking with each other, and she couldn't help but watch them, wishing she'd known them a lot longer. They were amazing together, one big happy family. Zoe came out with Raoul, joining the group.

"Maria," Daisy said, shouting her name.

Her cheeks heated as everyone turned toward her.

"Looks like someone's in trouble," Landon said.

Zoe slapped him around the back of the head. "Leave her alone."

She saw the deep friendship between the two, and Landon laughed, pulling her into his body for a hug. "Love you, too."

"Leave my girl alone before I kill you," Raoul said.

"Ugh."

"See, seriously alpha tendencies here," Landon said.

"I better go and see what he wants." Tucking her hair behind her ears, Maria made her way across the yard toward where Daisy stood near his bike. She hated how attracted she was to him. He was an asshole, and there's no way she should like him, and yet, she did.

Makes no sense.

Crazy body.

Crazy thoughts.

"Yes?" she asked, stepping in front of him. She forced herself to stare into his eyes. He'd been screwing another woman even after she'd told him she wanted a chance with him. Okay, so he hadn't exactly confirmed they were going to be in a relationship, but she'd opened up to him.

"We're going away for a couple of weeks, maybe even longer."

"Excuse me?"

"You, me, and we're going to see what happens."

She could only just stare at him. "Okay, you've completely lost me."

"We talked about being together. You becoming mine, and us exploring what we have together." He stepped closer toward her, but Maria held her ground.

"You've got to be kidding me right?" she asked.

"No, I've arranged for everything. We can leave now. Beth knows."

"I'm not going away with you. What we talked about a week ago no longer applies."

Daisy paused, rubbing his eyes. "Why?"

"Why? You think I don't know about the women you've been screwing?"

"They don't matter."

She snorted. "I don't care." She glanced behind her, and stepped close to him, inhaling his masculine scent. "I opened up to you. I gave you a chance, and it has been a damned week. You've been fucking other women, and that's it. Fuck all the women you like, I'm not going to give myself to a man who can't keep it in his pants." She wanted to be in a relationship where the man was in control, but there also had to be respect. Maria wasn't going to be some kind of doormat even though some people really thought that was going to be the case.

Maria went to walk away, but Daisy grabbed her arm. "I made a mistake."

"Guess what, I don't care." She pulled out of his hold and was about to march away, but Daisy stopped her. He moved in front of her, tossed her over his shoulder, and carried her toward his car.

"Get off me. Help! Help me!" She yelled for anyone to come and help her.

No one came rushing to her rescue. They simply laughed and waved.

She wasn't scared. Maria was angry, and she started thumping his ass, even though it was a very nice ass, with her fists.

He dumped her into the car, and she tried to climb out of the car only for him to have locked it already.

Beth came out of the main clubhouse and gave her a wave. It was a waste of time fighting. Folding her arms, Maria slumped down in her chair, feeling like a child. She was hurting, and yes, she was jealous, so damn jealous of the other women he was with.

Chapter Two

Daisy glanced across the car toward the woman who had literally flipped in his arms. Fucking hell, Maria had a lot of fight inside her. He also knew he'd hurt her. "I'm sorry," he said, giving her another look.

"I don't want to hear it. I'm not interested in you."

She wiped under her nose, and he felt like the world's biggest asshole as tears filled her eyes.

"I'm a jerk."

"Yes, you are. I told you that I wanted a man to take charge. I know we weren't a couple, but I told you what I wanted to give you. I wanted to give you everything, Daisy, and what did you do? You went and fucked other women. The club whores who screw anyone. How would you have felt if I'd jumped into bed with Landon? Or Knuckles? Or anyone else in the club?"

He gripped the steering wheel even tighter, gritting his teeth. "I wouldn't have liked it."

"I told you what I crave, what I want, and what I need. I accept that I'm not a conventional woman, but I'll only ever give myself to a man I trust. I'm not going to sit back and let someone be unfaithful."

Daisy listened to her and knew he'd made a mistake. "I've been part of the Trojans for a long time. I tried the whole girlfriend thing five years ago. I don't do relationships—"

"Then take me back to the clubhouse. I'm not interested in sharing, or having more than two people to a relationship."

"I'm not going to take you back."

"But you just said—"

"I know what I said. Look, I fucked up. What you're offering me, I tried once before. The woman I was with, she didn't consider me all that good. She believed I was controlling, and that no woman wanted a man like me. So I stopped hoping and craving, taking the release I needed out of the club women. This is all new to me."

Maria growled. "You're treating me like I was some other woman? Great, thanks, Daisy."

He pulled up against the nearest curb, and slammed his fist against the wheel. "Fuck, fucking, fuck." This was not going exactly as he hoped.

Turning to stare at the woman who had him all tied up in knots, he glared at her. Her raven hair cascaded all around her, contrasting with her pale skin. She'd been in the sun a lot, but she still hadn't tanned. He loved her silky soft skin. Her blue eyes shot fire at him, and filled him with warmth. Every time she looked at him, she heated him up from the inside out.

Daisy couldn't recall a time when a woman had affected him like this. She twisted him in knots, made him want shit that he'd forced deep inside.

"Do you want me to take you back to the clubhouse?" When she went to answer, he placed a finger over her lips. "Remember, this will be it between us. No going back, and I'll not ask you to consider this again. We'll be done."

He didn't know what to expect from her. Would she demand he take her back, or give him another chance?

She bit her lip and turned to face the road ahead. He'd give anything to be inside her head.

"If we do this, you've got to promise me there's not going to be any more women, Daisy," she said.

"There won't. Before, we didn't make any commitments. You told me something, and I reacted badly. I'm here now, and there won't be any other women. I will be faithful."

"One month, to see where this goes?" she asked.

"That's what I'm figuring. I'm not going to pressure you. We've got to get to know each other, and I figured we'd do that away from the prying eyes of the club."

"What happens when we get back?"

His mouth was dry. This had to be the craziest start to any relationship he'd been in. "Let's just handle today."

She nodded, rubbing her hands down her thick thighs. Fuck, he'd had so many dreams of her wrapped around his cock, squeezing his hips as he pounded inside her. His cock thickened just over the thought of being with her. Without caring that she was looking at his dick, he moved it to a more comfortable position.

"What the hell are you doing?"

"You made my dick hard. It's uncomfortable." He wasn't going to change who he was.

Chancing a quick glance at her, he saw her cheeks were flushed. "I can't believe you did that."

"I'm not some virgin, Maria. I like sex, and I'm not going to pretend that I'm not comfortable in my own skin."

"I'm a virgin."

"I know. We're going to break down those insecurities and build you back up." Daisy opened a window as it suddenly started to get a little too hard to think. Her feminine scent seemed to cling to every part of the car, invading his senses.

"I don't have insecurities."

"If I pulled up at a diner and I asked you to hand me your panties after you go to the toilet, would you?"

"No!"

"Then you've got insecurities, and I want you to do exactly as I say. I'll want to dress you how I want, and to be available to me. I'm not going to hold back."

There she went biting her lip once again, and he saw a diner up ahead. Time to test his theory. Parking his car, he pulled up the hand brake, and turned toward her. Cupping her face, he turned her toward him, pulling on the lip that was between her teeth.

"You make me want to bite that fucking lip." Leaning forward, he took her lip between his teeth, giving it a playful tug. In the next second he covered her mouth, claiming the kiss he'd been wanting since the first moment he saw her pull up at the Trojans MC clubhouse. She was fucking sweet, and she made him yearn to be the right man for her. Sliding his tongue across her bottom lip, he waited for her to gasp, so that he could plunder her mouth. He was going to fuck her pussy like this.

He'd take her cherry with his cock first, and then he was going to lick her sweet cunt with his tongue. His mouth watered for a chance to taste her sweetness. She'd be so damn good to taste. Stroking her cheek, he deepened the kiss, wanting to consume her, and never let her go.

Pulling away, he saw her eyes were closed, and she leaned a little closer to get him to kiss her.

"Let's go and eat." Climbing out of the car, he made his way around the car, opening her door. He took her hand and helped her out.

"I'm not hungry."

"I am, and you can keep me company while I eat." He kept hold of her hand as they walked into the diner. Daisy was still wearing his Trojans leather cut, and he was never going to take it off.

They took a seat toward the back, and Maria glanced around. "They're staring."

"Trojans carry a bad rep, babe. They're going to look, and be worried. They can keep on looking." He grabbed a menu and opened it up.

Maria moved around the table and took a seat beside him.

"You're not going to ask me to remove my jacket?" he asked.

"Why would I do that?" She looked up at him.

"You said people were staring."

"And you said that people can stare. I love your jacket. I'm not going to ask you to remove something that's hot." She shrugged. "If they're uncomfortable, tough."

She'd surprised him, and that was hard to do.

Smiling at her, he wrapped his arm around her shoulders, tugging her against him. "I want you to go into the bathroom, and remove your panties. Bring them back to me."

"How?"

"Take your jeans completely off, remove your panties, put your jeans back on, and bring them to me."

"I know how to take my panties off."

Her cheeks were flushed, and the bra she wore wasn't padded. He got a good shot of her full rounded tits and pointed nipples. She really was amazing. Daisy couldn't wait to get his mouth on her. He'd spend hours sucking her nipples, and biting on them. Would she like just a little pain?

She took a deep breath, but got up from the table.

"I'll order for us."

Maria nodded but didn't look back.

He admired her ass while she walked away. Daisy wanted to bite her ass, and sink inside her hot little body.

Virgin body.

No matter what he thought, he was a doomed man. He wanted her, and there was nothing he could do about that. There was a chance that he'd be able to get everything he ever dreamed of, and he wasn't going to screw it up.

****

Maria sat on the toilet and fought the battle inside herself. Part of her wanted to tell him to fuck off, but it was the same part of her that told her she had to, right? Women had a right to stand up to men, and to demand they see them as something more. She'd heard girls during high school, and even listened to other women talking about how they'd put their men in their place.

I'm so confused.

Taking her panties off would give her pleasure as much as it would Daisy.

Toeing off her shoes, she removed her jeans and panties. Placing her panties in her pocket, she zipped up her jeans.

Leaving the toilet, she walked toward the sinks and stared at her reflection. Her hair was pulled back into a ponytail, and her cheeks were flushed. Splashing her warm cheeks, she tried to cool them down, but nothing was actually happening.

"I can do this."

She wanted to do this.

Stop thinking about what others say you should want.

This is what you *want.*

You want to belong to Daisy.

For as long as she could remember she'd been intrigued by Daisy. Staying with Beth over the summer had allowed her the chance to feed her addiction for his friend's brother.

I'm evil.

She'd spent a great deal of time daydreaming about him.

Stepping out of the toilet, she saw Daisy was sipping from a cup.

I can do this.

We're exploring this together, and it's going to be fun.

Fun?

Since being at the Trojans MC clubhouse, she'd not contacted her parents. They cared about her, but they were so consumed by each other that they probably didn't notice that she was gone.

Taking a seat at the table, he nodded toward the tall glass. "I got you a chocolate milkshake."

Her heart started to pound as she stared at the tall glass with the frothy milkshake and the pink straw poking out of it.

Chocolate milkshake was her favorite.

"How did you know?" she asked, touched.

Daisy leaned in close so that his lips were close to her ear. "Do you really think I've not noticed you?"

Glancing over at him, she saw that he was studying her.

"What?"

He smiled. "I've been watching you, Maria. I know a great deal about you."

"Like what?" she asked.

"First, give me your panties."

She didn't even try to bargain with him. Maria handed him her panties as discreetly as she could, looking around the room to see if anyone was watching them.

No one was giving them a second glance. They must have gotten over Daisy's jacket.

"Good girl." He pocketed them, and took another sip of his coffee, black, with four sugars. She'd watched him pour himself a cup enough times. "You don't like peas, mushrooms, or canned fish. You like everything that is fresh, and you've got an addiction to spices. Chocolate and raspberry is your favorite combination, and you also happen to like vanilla ice cream." When she thought he was going to stop, he didn't. "You prefer flat shoes even though you can never reach anything on the top shelf. Nor do you like having your toenails painted, yet you allow Beth to do it as it relaxes her. You love children and enjoy taking care of them. Your favorite color is pastel blue, and you don't like wearing sun lotion. Christmas and the winter is your favorite time of the year. Do you want me to go on?"

"How do you know all this stuff?" she asked, shocked.

"I know a hell of a lot more. You love making friends even though it scares you. I also know you love the club, and you're comfortable around them. They're like a family, but they'll never hurt you."

Biting her lip, she couldn't help but stare at him, wondering about that small kiss they'd shared in the car.

"You're thinking dirty thoughts. Whenever you're thinking something dirty, you get all flushed. It's a fucking hot look on you, and I want to see it more often. Stop biting your lip, and take a drink of your milkshake."

She reached for her drink and took a sip. The chocolate flavor was intense but not overpowering. She closed her eyes, taking her time to bask in the taste.

"Good?"

"The best," she said. "Thank you."

Maria was excited to see what else he'd ordered. Some of the men she'd dated back at home would order some alcohol or tea for her to drink, or worse, soda. She hated soda.

"Your panties felt wet. You're aroused." He'd turned so that she had his full attention.

"I don't know what to say to that."

"Tell me what aroused you."

She stared at her drink, trying to find a reason.

"Don't think of a lie. Tell me the truth."

"You." She answered as honestly as she could.

"Me."

"Yes."

He aroused her in ways that were not easily described. She didn't know what to do about it. Every other guy that she'd dated had left her feeling cold. Not Daisy. He got her hot, and she imagined doing stuff she'd never thought possible.

"Do you think that's weird?"

He shook his head. "No." He took hold of her hand, and placed it over his erect cock. "You arouse me all the time."

Daisy was rock hard. His cock pressed against the front of his jeans. She held him in her hand, and he reached out, pushing some strands of hair behind her ear. "This is going to make for an interesting time together."

She smiled. Maybe they could do this? Maria was nervous. Who wouldn't be? Daisy wasn't a small guy, and he was a member of the Trojans MC. He was a tough guy, but it wasn't just that. She'd never been with another guy. Sure, she'd been on dates, but nothing that had gone further than a tame kiss.

There hadn't been any rainbows or shooting stars. The world hadn't started to spin, and she'd not become so consumed with need that she'd forgotten who she was. That had all happened with Daisy. The one kiss in the car had taken her breath away. She'd forgotten about herself and where they were.

You've been in love with Daisy for a long time.

It was more than just love. They had a connection, something that was far deeper than she thought possible.

"I did this to you?" She squeezed his dick, and he groaned, leaning forward to press his head against hers.

"Yes."

"What about all of those other women?"

"No one arouses me the way you do."

"How is that possible when you've spent more time fucking other women?" He hadn't pulled away from her, and she opened her eyes to stare into his.

"You said the word fuck. Pretty fucking hot." He licked his lips. "I can't wait to get you to say all kinds of nasty shit to me while I'm fucking you."

Maria smiled. "You really can't help it, can you?" She didn't mind the way he was. Her parents would talk about Daisy as the "*bad seed*", but she'd liked everything about him. He wouldn't fall in line, and he wouldn't do as he was told. There were plans made for him, which she'd heard about. Daisy, if he'd not gone and joined the MC at eighteen, would have made it through college top of his class. He wasn't stupid.

All of the plans had gone to shit the moment he walked away from his family.

"Do you want me to change?" he asked.

"No." Reaching out, Maria hesitated for a second, and then laid her hand on top of his leather jacket. "Like your jacket, I don't care what other people think."

"What are you thinking?"

"Can I ask you a question?"

"Sure, babe."

"Why did you not go to college?"

Daisy sighed. "You heard about that?"

"Your parents talked about it a lot. They constantly told Beth about what was happening, and what she should do."

Daisy cut her off laughing. "That's exactly why I stopped. They were busy making plans for me. I didn't want to have plans made for me, Maria. This life is my own, and I'm not going to live it through someone else."

"So you ran?"

"No. I'd heard about the Trojans when I'd left town. I'd come to Vale Valley for a party. It was when Russ was still in charge as the Prez of the club. I went, partied, and I saw how they were all together. They were strong. They were banded together as brothers. No one controlled them. They did what they wanted and didn't care what others thought. It's exactly what I want."

"They offered you what the college never did?"

"I love my parents, and Beth, but they expected me to go to college, become a partner in a firm." Daisy stopped, laughing. "They had my entire life mapped out. It wouldn't even shock me if they had a woman lined up for me to be my wife."

"It doesn't bother you?"

"Not now. I'm used to my parents being disappointed. I can't be that bad. I was the first person they contacted to take Beth."

Maria couldn't argue with him. "Beth loves you. She misses you all the time."

"I miss her. She was the only one who wasn't disappointed by my decision."

"Your parents still love you."

"I know that. Are you going to tell me what's going on with Beth?"

She shook her head. "Beth's secrets are not mine to tell. I wish they were. I'd tell you. She'll tell you when you're ready."

"Okay."

They were interrupted from talking as a waitress walked toward them. "Here's your pancakes with extra bacon and syrup."

She stared down at her plate, and couldn't help but be touched once again. Daisy knew a lot more about her than her own parents.

Chapter Three

Daisy parked the car outside of the single cabin in the forest. He'd followed the dirt path toward his one sanctuary in the world.

"Where are we?" Maria asked, looking around.

"We're at a vacation resort. A few years ago I saw this cabin up for sale online, and with it being in an abandoned location, I snapped it up."

Every single brother had a place to get away from the club. Not only did each of them have a secret location, it was also a safe house for all of them. Daisy's cabin wouldn't house every single club member, but he'd get between five and ten men, women, and children here.

"A vacation resort?"

Climbing out of the car once again, he rounded the vehicle to help Maria out. Wrapping his arm around her waist, he turned her so that she could see down the line of trees.

"There are more cabins."

"This is an exclusive resort that allows visitors to come and spend time being one with nature. Sometimes, like with my cabin, it allows some places to be bought so people can get away."

"You bought this?"

"Yes. I come here when I need to think." Turning her toward the main forest, he pointed down a certain path. "They have tour guides who are qualified to take people around the forest, looking over the wildlife. Getting back to nature is more popular now than ever."

"It's beautiful."

"Close your eyes, and listen." He did the same and listened to the open air. In the distance he heard the water near a local river, birds chirping, the trees moving from the slight breeze. *Peace.* "Come on, I want you to see the cabin."

"How long has it been since you were here?" she asked.

"A few months. Lucinda, one of the women who works as a tour guide, keeps an eye on the cabins. She makes sure they're cleaned and ready to receive their owners."

"She has a key?" Maria asked.

He heard the jealousy in her voice. "No need to be jealous, baby. Lucinda is in love with the man who owns all of the land here."

She relaxed a little in his arms.

"I've got you," he said, kissing the side of her neck. Guiding her toward the main door, he took out his key and slid it into the lock.

Maria reached up, taking the small white envelope that had been taped to the front of the door. She handed it to him, and he shook his head. "Open it, and read it."

"Daisy, I've cleaned the cobwebs, chased the spiders, and filled your fridge. Enjoy, and I hope your ladylove likes the resort. See you on a trail if you have time. Lucinda."

The curtains were drawn closed. Releasing Maria from his hold, he moved toward the curtains, allowing light to come into the cabin. He took care of the three sets of curtains in the sitting room, while Maria did the same in the kitchen. The cabin had three bedrooms, a main sitting room with a small dinner room at the back of the room, a bathroom, and kitchen. It was a modest cabin, and he loved it.

"It's beautiful," Maria said, looking around her space.

"I'm going to grab our things."

Leaving Maria to look around the small room, he grabbed their bags out of the trunk. After he'd been talking to Beth, he got his sister to pack a bag for Maria. He didn't doubt Maria would fight him. He'd dumped her bag in the trunk of the car while she'd been distracted by Holly and Mary. His club was amazing for creating a distraction when he needed it.

Before he'd gone to Duke asking for this time away, Holly and Mary had cornered him in the kitchen. Together, the two women had put some pretty harsh perspective on his situation. If he didn't claim Maria soon, she was going to be taken by someone else. The thought of another man taking what belonged to him filled him with rage. Maria was his woman.

Mine!

He wanted to possess every part of her so that Maria couldn't think or do anything without thinking of him first. Entering the cabin, he saw Maria was looking through the kitchen cupboards and checking out the use by dates on the tins.

Daisy closed the door and flicked the lock into place. Unless he went toward the main part of the resort, everyone knew to leave him alone.

Maria turned around, looking at the cases, then at him. "When did you have time to pack?"

"When you were busy doing something else." He folded his arms, and stared at her.

Her hands fisted at her sides.

Tugging the panties out of his pocket, he held them up. He inhaled her musky scent, and he wanted a taste of her.

Dropping the panties to the floor, he kicked out of his shoes, and removed his leather cut.

"What are you doing?" she asked.

"I'm going to get naked, and I want you to as well."

Her hand went to her chest, holding her shirt tightly.

Daisy stopped getting undressed. "I'm not going to fuck you. We're not going to do anything but look at each other."

"Why?"

"I don't want you nervous around me. I want to get naked. When I'm here, I don't abide by the laws of society, Maria. I get naked, and I enjoy being free." He started removing his clothes once again, getting naked for her to see. When he'd removed his shirt, and he stood in his jeans, he paused, and waited. "I'm not going to continue until you start taking some clothes off."

"I've never been naked in front of anyone."

"I'm not going to tell anyone. You're safe here with me, Maria. Here, it's just you and me. No club, no friends, no one else. We're alone to be who we are."

"What if you don't like my body?"

Sighing, he removed his jeans, and he wasn't wearing any boxer briefs himself. Wrapping his fingers around his cock, he stared at her. "This is how hard you make me, and you're not even naked. Start taking your clothes off, and see what you think."

"How are you going to handle that being hard?"

"I'm not some teenage boy. I can control my dick. You're not ready for me, and to be honest, babe, I'm not ready for this. I'm going to take my time, and we're going to get to know each other without anyone watching us."

She licked her lips and started to remove her clothes. Releasing his cock, he watched her start to bare even more skin. She kept her bra on as she removed her jeans, and he couldn't help but smile as she clearly forgot that she wasn't wearing any panties. Her pussy was covered in fine hairs, and soon he was going to take the time to shave her, have her smooth to the touch.

"Take your bra off," he said, wanting her naked.

Maria reached behind her back, and released the clasp of her bra. Her full, heavy tits were finally on display, and her body was better than he'd ever thought possible. She was full, curvy, and soft in all the right places.

Women were so hung up on being super slender, and all bones. He'd been with enough skinny women, and he appreciated the sight before him.

"See, baby, I'm already turned on by you, and you're fucking amazing."

She clasped her hands in front of her body, and stared at his cock. "What do you want me to do now?"

"Come here. Come and stand in front of me."

Maria bit her lip like she did every single time she was nervous. Slowly, she took the steps toward him, and the anticipation just kept on building inside him. Finally, after what felt like a lifetime passed, she was in front of him.

"What now?"

"Do you always want to have everything explained to you in little details, or do you want to actually enjoy what we're going through?" he asked. She took a deep breath, and he cupped her cheek. "You've got to learn to trust me."

"Take it one step at a time."

"Yes." Bending down, he grabbed their bags. "Come and see the bedroom." He urged her forward, and he watched her ass move with each step she took. This was how he was going to be spending the next couple of weeks. They were away from the club, and she was all his. He didn't have to worry about Beth interrupting them, or the club getting in the way. Four weeks, thirty days, and he was going to live out his dream. He really hoped she wanted this to continue, and that they did in fact see eye to eye.

Entering the bedroom, he placed the bags on the bed.

"Wow, that is a huge bed." She sat down on the edge and gave it a bit of a bounce.

"It's damn comfortable, baby. Give it a real test." He moved to the other side, and jumped on it.

Maria giggled and did the same thing.

****

Beth looked at the clock and wondered how long it was going to take Daisy and Maria to get to wherever they were going. Tapping her fingers across the bar, she tried to get into her book to distract her, but nothing was happening.

Releasing a sigh, she bent the book open, putting an even bigger dent in the spine.

"What's wrong?" Knuckles asked, sitting beside her.

It was only early afternoon, and she wouldn't disappear to her room until after six. She always helped with the dishes, and then left the club to party while she was alone.

"I was just wondering when Maria and Daisy will call."

Knuckles looked up at the clock. "Give it another hour."

"Do you know where they're going?"

He tapped his nose. "That would be telling. Don't worry. Daisy will take care of Maria. You don't need to think about what is going on there."

"I'm not worried. I know Daisy won't hurt Maria. He cares about her." She wasn't blind, and had seen the way her brother looked at Maria when he didn't realize someone was watching him. Daisy always looked at Maria as if he was a kid looking at his favorite toy but had been told he couldn't play with it. Maria wasn't a toy, but Daisy really wanted to play with her.

"That's something we can both agree on."

She stared at her book, hoping the words would register on her mind.

"Stop pretending to read the book."

"How do you know I'm not reading the book?" she asked, turning toward the man beside her.

Knuckles was large and dominating, but what surprised her was how she felt safe when she was near him. All of her fears evaporated when he was around. Even now, she no longer worried about Daisy and Maria while he was near.

"You've spent a lot of time looking at the clock on the wall. You're not kidding me that you're actually paying attention to the book."

Closing the book, she placed it down on top of the bar.

"You're right."

"I'm right about a lot of things." He reached out, and his finger stroked across her hand. "You can trust me, Beth. You can trust me with anything."

She tensed up, cutting off the thoughts of her demons, and shoving them away. No one could help her. The nightmares still came at night. Even if they were not as intense, they still came to her. She didn't want to go back home. Beth wanted to stay here so she never had to face the monsters waiting for her.

Her parents hated having to deal with the folk in town. Everyone knew the truth, and yet everyone was scared to speak up for fear of the consequences. She hated it.

"You're not ready to talk."

"If I was going to talk to anyone it was going to be my brother."

Knuckles laughed. "You're too good to lie. You and I both know that you're not going to tell Daisy."

"You think you're much better?"

"No. I'm not. I care, Beth, and if you tell me your secrets, they'll be between us." He captured her chin and turned her head so she had no choice but to look at him. "You can trust me."

She did trust him, and that was what scared her. All summer Knuckles had been there in the background whenever she was close to having a panic attack, or ready to hurt herself. He'd be there, talking, and slowly, the darkness inside her would ease. He took everything away, and she felt like her old self once again.

"I don't want to go back home," she said.

"Then what do you want to do?"

"I don't know. I like being here."

"You're not club whore material."

She wrinkled her nose.

"You're old lady material, babe." He covered her hand with his. "And you can be whatever you want to be, no matter how strange it may seem. You're a fighter. Whatever has you running scared, fight it. Don't let it win."

"Beth, Daisy's on the phone," Duke said.

Pulling her hand away from Knuckles, she walked toward Duke's office. The Prez of the Trojans held open the door, giving her enough room to pass. She couldn't resist another glance toward Knuckles. He gave her a wave, and she bit her lip.

What was it about him?

****

"Daisy doesn't want you sniffing around his sister while he's gone," Duke said, taking a seat at the bar.

Knuckles smirked. He knew Daisy was very protective of his sister. He couldn't blame him. If Knuckles had a sister, he'd have warned her against himself as well. He wasn't a good man, nor was he a kind man. Throughout his life, he'd used women and tossed them aside when another new pussy had appeared on the scene. He loved variety in the women he fucked, and didn't give a fuck who he hurt as he went through them.

Three of the club whores at the club were in love with him, or at least they were in love with his special toys that he liked to play with. He fucked them, and left them. He never offered them anything more than an orgasm, his cock, and about an hour or two of his time.

"I'm not going to do anything to Beth."

Now Beth, she was causing him some serious problems, and he didn't know what to do about that. She was twisting him up in knots, and making it hard for him to think clearly. The club whores had lost their appeal. At nighttime he struggled to forget about her. He'd try to use the club girls, but knowing Beth was somewhere close made it impossible for him to just sink into a willing cunt.

"Good. I don't want to have to deal with brothers fighting."

"We're not fighting over the same girl."

"No, you're fighting over his sister. You've got to show respect, Knuckles."

"I'm not going to hurt her. I'm not going to do anything that she doesn't like." Something had hurt Beth, and he was going to make sure that nothing ever touched her again. He couldn't have her, but it didn't mean that he couldn't keep her safe.

****

"You took long enough to call," Beth said. "I already told Daisy I'm going to kick his ass. What's your excuse?"

Maria smiled, hearing the fire in her friend. It had been too long since she'd heard her friend be that concerned before.

"You missing me?"

"Stop evading the question."

"We only just got here, and Daisy is just getting something ready for lunch." The scent coming from the kitchen was actually making her want to vomit. Daisy may have many good qualities, but cooking didn't seem to be one of them.

"Daisy's cooking?"

"I don't know if that smell can be called cooking. He's doing a science experiment in the kitchen."

"I'd keep the phone close in case he gives you food poisoning." Beth started to laugh, and Maria simply enjoyed the sound of her friend finally loosening up.

"How are you?" Maria asked.

The laughter faded. "I'm doing okay."

"You're sure?"

"Yes. You don't need to worry about me. What you need to worry about is having a good time with my brother. Speaking of Daisy, is he being nice?"

Rolling her eyes, Maria rested against the back of the bed. She was still completely naked, and she let out a sigh. "We've only been here a couple of minutes, not long enough to make an impression on each other."

"Be careful, Maria. I know you've been in love with Daisy for a long time. He's not the falling in love kind of guy."

Maria nodded. "I know."

"I don't want to see you hurt."

"What's going on with you?"

"Nothing. I was just talking with Knuckles. What do you think of him?"

She had seen Knuckles watching Beth. He'd not been looking at her with hunger. When Knuckles looked at Beth, it was like her was trying to figure her out. Beth was a puzzle he needed to solve. "He seems like a nice guy."

"All of the guys are nice here."

They were all nice because Beth was Daisy's sister, and he was part of the club. They were showing them some respect. She had no doubt that if they were just plain old party girls, they'd have been treated differently.

Maria had taken the time to observe the club whores, and the old ladies. Without even knowing the proper lingo, she saw the difference in the two groups of women. The club whores were used. She'd seen men at parties grab women, bend them over a surface, and fuck them.

Yes, she had sneaked out of her room to see what all the fuss was about. Hidden, she'd seen some of the men create a line behind one woman, and each man take her, spilling his cum into a condom, before another man took his place. The club did practice safe sex. She imagined that had to do with Crazy, and what happened to him. Crazy had been tricked by a club whore to the point that he'd gotten her pregnant, and ended up marrying her for the right to have the kid.

When it came to the club whores, once the men had their pleasure, they left the women alone. No emotion, no affection, nothing. It was like the women didn't exist. Now, the old ladies, that was completely different. They were not used in front of the club, and when they were close to their men, they couldn't keep their hands to themselves. Each man found a way to touch his old lady, be it a kiss, a touch of the hand, pulling her against him. They all tried to do it. Duke tended to grab the back of Holly's neck and kiss her. Maria always yearned for something like that, strong, possessive, and dominant. She had seen the way the men were with old ladies and the respect other men gave the women. Maria thought about Landon and Zoe. The two were friends, and Zoe belonged to Raoul. Even though Landon would tease Zoe, she'd seen the way he took care of her. No one could mess with an old lady and get away with it.

Maria wanted that. She wanted to belong to someone, and to have the respect of the club to know she belonged to one man.

"They're not all nice," Maria said. She was concerned about Beth, scared for her after what her friend went through.

"I'm not going to be stupid, Maria. You don't have to worry about me."

"I can't help but worry about you."

Beth sighed. "I'm not going back."

"You've made your mind up?"

"Yes. I'm not going back, and I'm going to call my parents up and tell them I'm staying here. I want to find something for myself."

Maria ran her fingers through her hair, trying to think of the best advice to give to her. Beth had been to hell and back, and she didn't want to be a cause for her friend to deteriorate.

"Benedict will pay one day, Maria. It won't be today, or tomorrow. It probably won't even be this year, but one day he will get what is coming to him," Beth said, whispering the words.

"Will there be justice for you?" Maria asked.

"It doesn't matter about me."

Tears sprang to Maria's eyes. She'd been the one to find her friend that morning, and had tried to fight Benedict and his family. No one would take Beth's word against the Mayor's son. The town only knew what it wanted to know, not the truth. The truth the town was not able to cope with. Maria wondered what would happen if the Trojans turned up, and showed Benedict's family they couldn't be bought or silenced. It would never happen because Beth wouldn't let her tell Daisy.

"You've got to tell someone."

"You want me to tell my brother? Do you know what he'd do to him? I can't let Daisy go to prison because of me. I love my brother."

Maria wasn't an idiot. She knew the MC was a dangerous group of men, and Daisy had hurt people throughout his life, maybe even gone as far as killing them. If anyone in the world deserved Daisy's kind of wrath, it was Benedict. The bastard was smug, getting away with everything, and that fucking angered her.

"He loves you as well."

"I don't want to talk about this, Maria. I want you to enjoy your time with my brother, and just have some fun. You've been craving his attention for a long time, and he's finally given in."

"Fine, you won't talk about it, and I can't make you."

"I will phone you tomorrow to make sure you survive my brother's food." After saying goodbye, they hung up, and Maria stayed seated on the bed, staring down at the cell phone. She had been friends with Beth for as long as she could remember. They lived so close together that they had been inseparable. They even used walkie-talkies at night so they weren't alone. The night Beth had gotten hurt, Maria had been bed-bound with sickness, and unable to help her friend.

Wiping away the tears that had fallen, she got to her feet and made her way toward the kitchen. The stench of burnt food was already heavy in the air, and when she walked toward Daisy, she watched him jump back, cursing.

"Fuck! This looks fucking easy on the TV. What the fuck am I doing wrong? Lying bastards."

"What's wrong? Who lied?" Maria asked, doing her hardest not to laugh.

"Bloody chefs on TV. They make food look easy."

"They're supposed to. It's food, and it's their careers. They would make anything look easy."

"Are you just going to stand there, or are you going to help me?" he asked.

"Go, and sit." She pointed at the chair near the kitchen. "You need to stay as far away from the kitchen as humanly possible. I mean, seriously, look at the mess of the kitchen." She pulled the frying pan off the heat, and saw an egg, or what looked like an egg swimming in fat. *Ew.* It looked so gross, and her stomach turned.

"I was trying to do the right thing."

"It's nearly dinner." She shook her head, completely amazed that anyone could destroy a fried egg.

"I like fried eggs. I've watched Holly and Mary work."

She glanced toward him, seeing him pouting. "You're just a big cuddly teddy bear, aren't you?"

"No!"

"You're pouting. Who knew a Trojan could pout? It's kind of cute, and you're supposed to be this badass biker. I'm not scared of you, Daisy."

"I don't want you to be afraid of me, Maria. I want you to be turned on by me."

She paused, and turned to look back at him.
"What?" She had to have heard wrong, right? Daisy had
never crossed that line with her, well, apart from being
completely naked in front of her.

He leaned back in his chair looking every part the
sexy biker. "Tell me, Maria, is your pussy wet?"

"You're asking me this now, when we've got
food to cook?"

Daisy shrugged. "I'm a man who likes his food,
and his pussy. You want to belong to me then you've got
to be honest with me. Is your pussy soaking wet?"

She stood before him naked, and he was asking
her about her pussy. Daisy hadn't put any clothing on,
and as he sat back, he wrapped his fingers around his
swelling cock.

"This is all for you. Come here."

Food could wait. Any hunger she had disappeared
as Daisy became her main focus. She took her time
making her way over to him. His legs were partially
open, and he slid them open a little more, waiting for her
to step between them.

"I love the fact you're not embarrassed about
being naked."

She hadn't thought about being naked. Daisy
made her lose focus of all of her insecurities, and her
thoughts were on him. He invaded her mind, and the heat
in his eyes left her in no doubt that he was attracted to
her. She loved the way he stared at her. For the first time
in her life, she felt empowered, in control, and ready for
life.

He placed his hands on her hips, and she couldn't
resist biting her lip. His touch alone had her aroused.

"Your nipples have gotten hard, babe. You like
my hands on you?"

She didn't bother to lie, and nodded her head whispering the word. "Yes."

Daisy ran his hands from her hips up to just under her breasts. She couldn't help but take a breath in. His touch made it impossible for her to concentrate on anything else.

Chapter Four

"You know what I love about being here?" Daisy asked, rubbing his thumbs across the underside of her tits. Her nipples were rock hard, pushing up, and begging to be sucked. Her body was so damn curvy, and he just wanted to touch, caress, and arouse her.

"No, I don't."

"I can have you naked all day, every day." He ran his thumbs across her nipples again, giving in to his pleasure. Just touching Maria was all it took for him to get aroused. His cock was straining to get inside her. He also loved how damn responsive she was. Maria didn't hold anything back, opening herself up to his touch, and loving it. "No brother will see you."

"No one?"

"No one. You're all mine. I don't like sharing, Maria."

She opened her eyes and stared at him. "You're lying. I've seen you share."

"When?"

"At the clubhouse. It's not like there is a lock on my door keeping me out. I've left my room, and saw you fucking other women. One after the other the men use them." She held onto his shoulders. "You've no problem with sharing then."

"There's a huge difference."

"What?" she asked.

"None of those women belonged to me. They're club property. They fuck every single guy in the club, and they love doing it. You came to me, Maria." She was old lady material, through and through. "No other man will ever know how damn big your tits are, or how your nipples pucker when you're aroused." Sliding one hand from her ribcage down her stomach, he cupped her between her thighs. "They'll never know how soft your skin is, or how wet you can be." He slid his finger between the lips of her pussy, and Maria tensed up. "No one touched you here before?"

She shook her head.

You're the first man.

There's a chance for you to be the only man.

Daisy filled with excitement at the prospect of being the only man to touch, explore, and eventually fuck Maria.

Sliding his finger across her clit, he saw her shake, and her nails dug into his shoulders. "You're not used to being touched, my little virgin."

Cupping her breast, he matched the strokes over her clit with her nipple. Maria closed her eyes, and he didn't want that. He wanted her eyes on him all the time. "Look at me."

She opened her eyes, and the blue in her depths seemed a little deeper.

Pulling his fingers away from her pussy, he held his finger up between them. "You're soaking wet for me." Grabbing her hips, he stood up. He was much taller than Maria, and her head only came to his chest. "I want you on the table."

He helped her onto the table, and pressed his fingers to her chest. "Lie back."

"Why?"

"Do you trust me?"

"Yes."

"Then trust me when I say lie back."

Maria sighed, and slowly lowered her body to the table. Standing at the head of the table, for the first time, Daisy felt like the king of his castle. Maria had always been his woman, and he'd been fighting it for so long. The moment she came to the clubhouse with his sister, he should have claimed her as his own. Instead, he'd waited. She was younger than he was by ten years, but he wouldn't ever stop her from living life. She was nineteen, ready for college, and everything else that the world could offer her. He wanted her to have everything her heart desired, including him.

Would you give her up if she wanted a man without the club?

Daisy gripped her hips, and pulled her to the edge of the table. She didn't want what other people wanted. Maria, herself, had told him that. She wanted him, to belong to him. There had to be a way that they could both find what the other wanted.

I've got some time.

His sister wasn't going anywhere. She'd already told him that she didn't want to leave Vale Valley. He hadn't questioned the reason behind his sister's decision. If Knuckles had anything to do with it, he honestly didn't know what to do. On the one hand, he wanted to thank Knuckles for keeping his sister close to him. Then of course, on the other hand, he wanted to kill Knuckles for even trying to encourage Beth. It was a two edged sword.

"You've been wearing those pretty little dresses all summer to tease me, to taunt me with what I can't have," he said, caressing his fingers down to her pussy. He opened her pussy lips and saw her swollen clit. She was so wet and creamy. He wanted a taste of her. The scent of her arousal was heady in the air. His cock strained up, and even though all he wanted to do was pound inside her, he held back. "The truth is, babe, this has always belonged to me."

"Yes."

He smiled. "Any man tried to kiss what belongs to me?"

"No."

"Do I need to kick someone's ass for touching my woman?"

"No. I'm yours, Daisy, all yours."

"I like that, baby. You're giving me something I've only ever dreamed about." He had his own virgin to train exactly how he wanted her. Daisy wouldn't hurt Maria. Sliding his fingers through her slit, he stroked over her clit, around, across, and over. She started to breathe long and deep. Her cheeks grew flushed as she stared back at him. "You're growing wetter."

"Are you going to—" She bit her lip, stopping what she was about to say.

"You've got to say the words, babe. I'm not going to even try to guess what you're going to say."

"Are you going to … fuck me?"

Damn, those words had his cock thickening even more. She didn't have any clue how damn sexy and hot she sounded, and it was driving him crazy with need.

"One day, I will. Today, tonight, it's not going to happen."

He wanted to get it so that she was so lost with her desire to fuck him that she was begging him every chance she got. Daisy was going to spend his time showing her how good it could be between the two of them.

You want to keep her.

That wasn't just it. His feelings for Maria were a lot deeper than that.

"You see, little Maria, there's a lot more fun to be had. I don't just have to fuck you, and get it over with. I can do a lot more than that." Using both of his hands, he placed both his thumbs on either side of her clit, and started to caress her. She arched up, moaning as he stroked her sweet pussy.

"Do you see what I mean, babe?"

"Daisy!" She screamed his name, sitting up on the table. Releasing her clit, he gripped her hair tightly, and slammed his lips down on hers, sucking her bottom lip into his mouth. He was ravenous, and the only person he wanted to taste was right in front of him. Her perfect body called to him, begging for him to take, to fuck, to love.

"You're mine," he said, growling the words against her lips, deepening the kiss further.

She gripped his shoulders, gasping out his name, and he devoured her mouth, needing to consume every part of her.

He let go of her hair, and started to glide his hands down her body, cupping her tits, then down even more.

"I've changed my mind. It's time for a taste of this creamy cunt," he said.

Taking a seat in his chair, he leaned forward, and slid his tongue across her clit, circling the bud, then gliding down to hover over her virgin entrance. He was going to claim that pussy, and mark every single part of her.

There was only one word that he thought about when he looked at Maria.

Mine.

****

Maria cried out as he sucked her clit into his mouth. He used his teeth, and she couldn't pull away, nor did she want to. His hands opened her pussy lips, sucking, flicking, and licking her clit. The pleasure was instant, and in that moment, she wondered why she'd never done this before.

No one is good enough.
No one but Daisy.

"You taste so fucking good, babe. I'm going to be sucking your clit a lot over the next couple of weeks.

53

Actually, scrap that. I'm going to be sucking your clit for the rest of my life." His tongue moved down, circling her entrance but not penetrating. Whenever his tongue moved toward her entrance, she tensed up expecting him to simply take her. "I told you I won't be fucking this pretty pussy, baby. You've got to learn to trust me."

Her cheeks heated as he continued to tease her.

This was what she wanted, what she craved.

Daisy flicked his tongue back and forth over her clit, and she just couldn't hold back her screams of pleasure.

The orgasm started to build inside her, and there was no way for her to stop her release, or fight it. There, on Daisy's kitchen table, she came, thrusting her pussy onto his face, and loving every second of his lips on her.

He didn't stop and kept on sucking her clit. The pleasure continued, taking her by surprise, and making her scream his name over and over. Finally, he slowed his strokes, and pulled away with a final kiss.

"You're fucking beautiful," he said, kissing her clit.

She took a deep breath and glanced down to find him licking his lips. Her cheeks heated from the hunger in his eyes.

"Tasty."

He stood up, and she caught sight of his erect cock. Daisy was rock hard, and the tip leaked his pre-cum.

"Do you want me to take care of that?" she asked.

"I'll take care of this. I want you to stay exactly where you are so I can admire the view." He wrapped his fingers around his dick, and worked from the base up to the tip.

Lifting up on her elbows, she looked down to watch him masturbate. His cock looked so damn hard.

"Does it hurt?" she asked.

"No, it doesn't hurt. It feels good. Just looking at you arouses me. Don't get me wrong, I said I won't fuck your pussy, but it doesn't mean I don't want to." One of his hands rested on her knees, and she opened her thighs wider for him to see. "When I take you and make you mine, you're not going to be in any doubt to how I feel about you."

"I want you, Daisy."

"You want me, but you're not ready for me. I'm not a small guy, and I've got to get you ready. There's a lot more to do, and have fun with than just going straight into fucking." He slowed his movements on his cock.

Maria tensed up as he placed his cock between the lips of her pussy, and started to move up and down. Each thrust of his hips had him bumping her clit. "What other things?" she asked.

"Like this. I'm not fucking you, but I can tell you I'm getting a shitload of pleasure right now just by watching you. You're driving me fucking crazy, baby."

He leaned over her, taking one of her nipples into his mouth and sucking hard. The pleasure and slight pain consumed her, making her arch up against him. The breast he wasn't suckling, he started to pinch the nipple, teasing her body.

Daisy pulled away, his thrusts growing more powerful as he grabbed her hips. He didn't fuck her, but it was so damn close.

"We've got a lot to explore together, to get to know each other. You've given me your trust, and it's time for me to show you what I can give you." He slammed his lips down on hers and grunted. She felt his cock pulse, followed by his cum spilling onto her stomach. Maria stared into Daisy's eyes as he came. He looked different, more masculine somehow.

"That was amazing," she said.

"There's a hell of a lot more for us to look forward to." He pressed another kiss to her lips, and stood. "Come on, baby, it's time for you to feed me."

He moved away, and she was about to get up when he came back with some tissues.

"What are you doing?" she asked.

"I'm cleaning you up." He wiped away his semen and helped her off the table. Daisy wrapped his arms around her waist, holding her up. Her legs were weak from the pleasure. He kept holding her until she was steady, and then he released her.

"I want to ask you a question," he said.

Maria tensed up, knowing it was going to be about Beth. She didn't know why she knew it was going to be about Beth, only that he sounded different when he was talking about her sister. "I can't tell you."

"Is it something I can help with?" he asked.

He looked torn, and so damn upset that she almost told him.

"Please don't put me in this position. Beth's my best friend, and you're … I don't know what you are."

Daisy sighed, looking like he wanted to argue.

"You're my woman, Maria. Don't forget that. I'll keep asking Beth, but I won't put you in the position that it'll call your friendship into question." He pressed a kiss to her head and stepped back.

"Go and make us some dinner. I've got a couple of calls to make."

Maria stood watching him as he walked away. He picked up his jeans, sliding them on. Daisy grabbed the cell phone and walked out of the cabin. She saw him on the cell phone in the next instant.

Why can't you trust him, Beth?

Beth's secrets were not hers, but she had a feeling if she didn't tell Daisy soon, it could cost her a relationship with him.

Chapter Five

"I'm sick and tired of this bullshit, Dad. What happened to Beth?" Daisy asked. He didn't want to put Maria in a difficult position, but he also needed to know what the hell was going on.

"Son, we asked you not to ask questions. Beth is getting better. She's even called us about her staying there indefinitely—"

"And you're happy with that? I remember when Beth wanted to go out of town to a college. You lost your shit. You didn't even want the club coming near her. The Trojans are the best kind of men, and now you're more than happy with her being around me all the time?" Daisy was really starting to get confused.

No one knew anything.

Go to the source?

What if he was to go to the town where his parents were? Take a couple of the guys, and just get a feel of the place? Even as he thought of it, he looked through the window and saw Maria standing at the stove. Her ass swayed, and from the sounds coming outside, she'd put some music on.

Fuck!

He'd have to do something when he got back home. This was his one chance with Maria, and he wasn't going to screw it up.

"Daisy, you need to stop talking about this. It's not your business, and Beth doesn't need that kind of shit here."

"You're kidding me right? Not my kind of business? My sister is a shell of her former self, and you don't think I need to know shit like that?" Daisy started to pace up and down, getting angrier with every passing

second. This entire situation was starting to piss him off.
No, it wasn't starting to. He was pissed off.

"Do you love Beth?"

"You know I do. She's my sister. I'd die
protecting her."

"Then accept that she doesn't want anything to
happen. She's happy with the Trojans, and you. Please,
for her, control yourself."

Daisy closed his eyes and counted to ten. His
anger was one of his problems. Once he started, it was
hard for him to keep it under control. He'd never hurt
anyone who didn't deserve it. He hadn't hurt a woman
before, either. There was a time when he was concerned
that he wouldn't be good for women.

No woman had inspired him to kill. He'd
witnessed that emotion in Crazy and Duke. Daisy had
only seen Duke actually kill a woman, not that he could
blame him. Duke's ex had almost killed Holly.

"I've spoken to Beth. She's said you're courting
Maria?"

Daisy chuckled. "You're trying to change the
subject?"

"Maria's always been in love with you. When
you're around, there's a sparkle in her eyes. I've never
seen that girl react to anyone the way she does to you."

He thought about the time he'd been with Maria.
When she was younger, he'd tried to avoid her. He'd
noticed her sidelong looks, and the way she stared at him.
Daisy had always assumed she'd not liked him, being
Beth's rebel brother.

How wrong he'd been.

Looking through the window, he saw Maria
singing into a wooden spoon, swinging her hips from side
to side. She really was something. He loved how she
wasn't embarrassed to be naked around him.

You were naked as well.

He doubted she'd have willingly gone without clothes if he'd not gotten naked as well.

His cock started to thicken once again, and he moved away from the window.

"Be careful with her, Daisy."

"Beth?"

"No, Maria. She's got a fire inside her that makes her seem strong, but I'd bet every cent I have that she's vulnerable, breakable."

Daisy didn't doubt it, and he wouldn't bet his small fortune either. Maria was vulnerable, and if she let him into her heart, and he broke it, it would shatter her. She was a strong woman in everything, but when it came to her heart, she was a kitten.

"I won't hurt her."

"Before you make her your old lady, or whatever you call it, make sure you're sure. I don't want you to get hurt, and to inadvertently hurt her either," his father said.

"Okay."

Daisy looked toward the door as Maria peered out. "Food is ready."

He nodded. "I've got to go."

"Think about what I've talked about."

Thinking about it wasn't the problem. What his father was trying not to say was don't act on what he'd said. Growing up Daisy had gotten into more trouble because he acted on his own thoughts.

Daisy wasn't a stupid man, and he knew the best way to deal with problems was to wait for them to go cold. If you reacted in the heat of the moment, there was no chance to enjoy the chaos that would come after. Daisy liked to enjoy taking down his problems, screwing them over and over again. There was nothing like prolonging the moment.

He hung up the phone, walking toward Maria. She looked so damn gorgeous—and naked. He quickly removed his jeans so that he was naked once again.

"Who were you talking to?" she asked.

"My dad."

"You were asking about Beth again, right?"

"Yes."

She sighed. "You're not going to let it go?"

"Would you, if it were your sister?"

"No. I wouldn't. You're a good brother, Daisy."

Taking hold of her hand, he tugged her toward him. He loved the way she melted against him, trusting him. "Have you always thought that?"

"Yes."

Cupping her cheek, he ran his thumb across her bottom lip. "You know, there was a time I thought you couldn't stand me."

Maria shook her head, sighing. "It just goes to show men don't know what they're talking about. You confused me. When I was younger, you always made me nervous, and I wasn't ready for what I wanted."

"Which is what?"

"You. You're not an easy person to ignore, Daisy. You've got a presence around you, and it's hard to just turn away. When you were around, my body seemed to have a mind of its own."

He tilted her head back. "You got turned on by me, baby?"

She smiled. "Yes. Dinner is ready."

"Let's go and eat."

Taking hold of her hand, he led the way back into the room. She followed without fighting him. He half expected her to fight him on something. She was a little firecracker to the core.

Two plates were on either side of the table, and he didn't like it.

Taking hold of one plate, he put it next to his. "I want you to sit beside me."

She took a seat next to him, shivering. "It's a little cold."

He burst out laughing.

"I don't know if this will be better than Holly and Mary's food."

"I don't compare, baby."

She winced. "That's not good, is it?"

"Do you want to know if your food is awful?"

"Yes. If things go well together, won't you want me to cook for you?" she asked.

Didn't she realize that even if her cooking was shit, he'd eat it anyway? Reaching out, he tugged some of her hair behind her ear.

What was it about her?

Love?

Sex?

Lust?

Maria had always made him think about who he was as a man. Was this what Duke, Pike, Raoul, and Crazy had gone through? All four brothers had recently found their old ladies. Holly, Mary, Zoe, and Leanna were amazing women. Maria, she was a wonderful woman, and she'd fit right in with the old ladies. The club would support and love her if something happened to him.

He trusted the club more than anything.

"Then I better have a taste." Finally looking down at the plate he saw there was some fettucine with marinara sauce.

"I used the spicy Italian sausage I saw in the fridge. There was a jar of marinara sauce, and I mixed it all together. I hope that's okay."

"It's fine, babe." It smelled amazing. The garlic, herbs, and spices from the sausage were making his mouth water. He stuck his fork in the center, and gave it a twirl. Once his fork was full, he took a large bite, and flavor exploded inside his mouth.

Now, Holly and Mary were damn good cooks. Leanna had the best lasagna, but he'd scored a woman who could cook, too.

Glancing toward her, he saw she was nibbling her lip and staring at him waiting. "If you don't like it, I'll go and cook something else."

"I love it, baby. This is fucking tasty."

"It's something Beth always liked as well."

"You cooked for Beth?" He didn't like the hit of jealousy that struck him.

"Yes."

Get over yourself. She's been with Beth for years.

Taking her hand, he locked their fingers together and started eating once again.

"I like cooking for you," she said.

Tightening his hold around her, he smiled. He liked her cooking for him as well.

****

"What's the matter, baby?" Holly asked, walking up behind him. They were out at their ranch, and Duke had just found Matthew sexting with a girl from high school. Sexting? What the fuck was sexting? Yeah, talking sex while texting, and he'd had enough with this shit with regards to his son. He got about growing up, but there was ways to do it. Duke didn't want Holly finding out what was going on, but his son seemed determined to make it known.

"It's about Matthew."

"What about him? He's doing his homework, right?" Holly asked, looking toward the dining room.

"He is."

"Are you going to talk to him about college? I don't want him to go away, but if it will give him the best possible start in life, I'd have to live with that."

This was what he loved about Holly. She was caring to the very core. Matthew was not her son, and yet she loved him as if he was.

"He's having sex." There, he'd said it.

Holly laughed. "So? What's the problem?"

Duke frowned. "Matthew. I caught him having sex."

"The kid's seventeen. He's your son, and I take it the girls he's with are the same age."

"Wait, what?"

"Matthew is a good kid, and he's not stupid either. I saw his stash of porn months ago. In fact, when we first moved in together, I saw it."

"Excuse me?"

"I thought you knew." She kissed his cheek and ruffled his head. "I'm going to go and take care of Drake. He's growing up so fast."

Three years had gone by so fast, and as he watched Holly walk out of his office, which he kept at the ranch, he wondered what had happened to the woman who would have been pissed off.

"Hey, Dad," Matthew said. "Now that you can see that Holly's got no issues, are you going to give me my phone back?" Matthew folded his arms across his chest, and smirked.

Duke sighed. "What happened to that little boy that was happy with a train set?"

Matthew rolled his eyes. "No one can stay young forever, Dad. I bet you were like this growing up."

Grabbing Matthew's cell phone from inside his desk, he walked around, flipping the phone between his fingers, and catching it. "You know, when I was your age, I didn't have this kind of technology, didn't even give a shit about it. Sexting wasn't a thing. I had a real woman in my hands, and I fucked her until she couldn't remember her own name."

Matthew held his hand out to take the phone. "I know what I'm doing."

"I'm going to let you have this phone with the agreement that you will take one year going to the college of Holly's choice."

"What?" Matthew frowned. "I want to prospect with the club. I want to be like you."

"Yet if given the option I'd have gone to college. The club life is in my blood, but I didn't have any other choice. You've got a chance to be something more."

"Suits don't get you the pussy."

Duke shook his head. Staring down at his son's phone, Duke didn't want to do what he was about to, but there was no choice. Matthew was showing a side to himself that wasn't going to go down well at the club, or in the world. He loved his son, and he was going to give him a harsh reality check.

Fisting the phone, he threw it with all of his force toward the wall. The phone shattered, dropping down to the floor.

"What the fuck, Dad?"

"You think you're being a smartass, but all you're doing is showing you're a kid with a dick that can get hard. Let me tell you something, Son, that hard dick will answer to the law. You knock up one of those girls, that will fall on you. You don't bag your shit, and someone's infected, you've got to live with that all your life." Duke laughed. "You want to have a shot at being a prospect, well congrats, kid, you've just been initiated." Duke would get his son a new phone, but he didn't see any other way in getting through to Matthew other than letting the harsh realities of prospecting speak for him.

****

The following morning, Maria opened her eyes and saw that the sun was streaming through the bedroom window. Behind her, Daisy snuggled up against her, and she couldn't help but sigh. Last night they had done the dishes together, and then watched some television, and a movie.

When the movie had finished, Daisy led her toward the bedroom, and he'd shocked her by spooning her.

"You're awake?" Daisy asked.

"How did you know?"

"Your breathing changed, and you got tense in my arms."

"I didn't know you were awake." She went to roll over, but Daisy stopped her.

"Don't. I want to hold you, and just wake up slowly."

Smiling, she placed her hands over his, liking how warm he was, surrounding her with his warmth.

"I enjoyed last night," she said.

"Me, too. You're the first woman I've spent the night just watching television with."

"Have you ever been in love with a woman?" she asked.

"No. I've never been in love. You?"

She shook her head. "No."

Caressing her fingers over his hand, she felt his cock pressing against her ass. He was getting harder with every passing second.

"Do you feel what you're doing to me?"

"Yes."

"I've imagined this," he said, surprising her.

"You've thought about being in bed with me?"

"Yes, and I can tell you that the reality is much better than the fantasy." He kissed her neck, moving up to bite her ear.

She gasped, moaning as pleasure rushed through her entire body.

"I've got plans for today, baby."

"You do?" She opened her thighs, ready for him to play with her.

"Yes, and it doesn't involve sex." He suddenly pulled away from her, and climbed out of bed. Her pussy was dripping wet, and his cock stood to attention. Still, he didn't stop, and moved toward the wardrobe.

"What are you doing?"

"Getting you some clothes."

She lifted up on her elbows and watched as he went through the clothes that had been packed for her, which she'd placed in the wardrobe last night. The clothes were next to his, and she got a thrill from seeing them side by side.

"Do you want to get your own clothes?" Daisy asked. His hand turned into a fist, and his movements seemed very precise as he dropped his hand beside his body, turning to look at her. What did she see in his eyes?

Something flashed beneath his depths. Confusion? Annoyance? Hope?

Was it some kind of test?

"You're the one who knows where we're going. You can pick. I don't have a problem with that." She smiled at him, admiring the full length of his body. His cock was still rock hard, and she liked how he seemed to ignore it.

Daisy had a confidence that surprised her.

He turned, giving her a full shot of his back and ass. His ass was firm, and she finally understood what Holly and Mary were on about when they talked about men's asses.

She watched as he pulled out of the wardrobe a pair of shorts that went to mid-thigh, along with a blue tank shirt. Next, he moved toward the drawers along the far wall where she'd placed her underwear.

Heat spilled from her pussy as she waited for him to finish. He walked back to the bed, carrying a bra and a pair of socks, placing them on top of the clothing.

"Where are we going?" she asked.

"You'll find out soon enough." He moved toward her side of the bed, cupping her hip as he leaned in close, pressing a kiss to her lips. "You're making breakfast?"

"Yes."

"Good." He pressed a kiss to her lips, and removed the blanket from around her as he did. "It's time for you to get dressed."

Daisy stepped away from her, and she saw that he went toward the wardrobe again getting his own clothes.

Stepping out of the bed, she made it before getting dressed. When she turned back to her clothing, she noticed Daisy's gaze on her. This *was* a test. Something in her gut was telling her that he was testing her, waiting to see if she would fail.

Straightening her shoulders, she reached for the shorts, not even questioning the lack of panties. Pulling the shorts up her thighs, she gave a stretch, waking up her body. There was a thrill to having Daisy watch her as she dressed. Not only was she getting excited from him watching, she loved the fact he'd picked out the clothes. The shorts, the shirt, and the bra, it was all what Daisy wanted her to wear.

Putting the bra on, she tugged the shirt on immediately after, and when she sat on the bed, to deal with the socks, Daisy caught her face between his palms. He tilted her head back, and she saw that he was assessing her as he stared at her. The jeans he wore were unbuttoned, and she liked the small patch of hair it revealed.

"You've surprised me."

"Why?"

"I didn't expect you to do that without an argument."

Feeling somewhat confident, she took hold of his face, smiling up at him. "I surprise myself." Pressing a kiss to his lips, she released a sigh. "I'm going to go and start us some breakfast."

"Will you make us up a small picnic hamper?" he asked.

"Yes, I will."

She took one last lingering look before making her way toward the small kitchen.

This is really happening.

Her heart was pounding, and her pussy was slick from what had just happened.

He only got your clothes.

It was more than the clothes. Daisy had given her something that he clearly wanted to do but had been pushed away. She saw the conflict.

Firing up the grill, she took out some bacon and eggs. While she was waiting for the grill to heat up, she grabbed out several items and started to make up some sandwiches for the rest of the day.

Once she had the bacon on the grill, she buttered some bread and started to make up a picnic basket, obviously without the basket.

Daisy entered the kitchen and put a picnic basket on the kitchen counter. "I found this."

"You already owned a basket?"

"It's something I like to go on."

"You like to go on picnics?"

He moved up behind her, placing a hand on her stomach, and tugging her back. "I like going for long walks with a woman I actually like. Also, I love food."

"We're going for a walk today?"

"I'd love to have you completely naked all day, and play with you. I didn't buy this cabin for us to just sit inside. It has beautiful scenery, amazing walkways, and I think you're going to love it. Also, there's a nice spot near a lake where you can watch deer, waterfalls, and offers tranquility."

"Will we see other people during our time out?"

"Maybe. It's always busy, and there's tour guides. We'll have to wait and see." He kissed her neck. "Are you looking forward to it?"

"Yes."

She really was. Maria loved going for long walks, and enjoying nature on her trips. Beth always found it annoying that she loved walking down the long beaches rather than lounging around catching the sun.

He gave her neck a nibble before stepping back. "I'll let you finish food." Daisy didn't walk out of the kitchen. He started to gather other items to place in the basket. Out of the corner of her eye, she saw him placing bottles of water at the bottom of the basket. He then placed a flat sheet down and started adding plastic cups and plates.

Focus, Maria, focus.

Finishing up their sandwiches, she placed them in the basket. She removed the bacon from the grill, scrambled them up some eggs, and buttered a few slices of toast. She was more than ready to eat.

Taking a seat beside Daisy, he held her hand as they ate together.

This was what she wanted. Was that wrong?

Chapter Six

Daisy couldn't stop himself from holding Maria's hand as they walked down the dirt path toward a thick set of trees. The picnic basket he held in his other hand was a little heavy, but he wouldn't have Maria carrying it. She was a beautiful woman, and every chance he got, he looked at the clothes he'd picked. Not once had she voiced a complaint. He didn't know what he expected, but it hadn't been her quiet acceptance. Still, that was exactly what he got.

"So, what are your plans?"

"Plans?" she asked.

"You know, when we get back to Vale Valley?"

"I don't know. Beth's told me she wants to stay in town, and I was thinking of staying with her. I'm not entirely sure yet what I want to do. Beth's been my friend for years, and now all of a sudden there's a chance we won't be together." She sounded sad.

"You don't have to leave Vale Valley." Daisy gritted his teeth as he stared ahead.

"I don't want to leave."

They were silent for several seconds, and ideas rushed around his head, waiting for one to stay on focus. "You ever thought about what would happen if we continued back at home?" he asked.

They had been walking around this for years, even before she was legal. Looking back now, Maria had always been there in his life even when he'd not realized it. He'd never try anything with an underage girl, not even Maria.

Stopping, Daisy turned toward her. She was nibbling her lip as she stared down the long path ahead.

God, I love this woman.

The thought struck him hard, taking the wind out of him. He took a deep breath and placed the picnic basket down on the ground.

"I don't know what you want me to say."

"Tell me what you're thinking," he said.

"Daisy, this is our second day together, and before that, you rebelled, going into the arms of another woman."

"Then let me have this month of proving to you that I can be faithful to you."

Maria chuckled. "We're alone in the middle of nowhere."

Shit!

"Then how about after we have some time here, getting to know one another, and settling this uncertainty between us, we go back. You can give me a test run."

She tilted her head to the side, looking at him. "You really thought I'd fail this morning."

"We're going all over the place right now."

"Then stop being vague, and tell me what your problem is." She tried to pull her hand away, but he held onto her, not wanting to let go. "Daisy?"

"I'm not letting go. Okay, I was in a relationship once. No, I wasn't in love, and while I was with this woman, I did what I did this morning. I picked out clothes, and I asked her to do certain things." He hated how fucking needy he sounded, and whiny. Daisy had gotten over Laura. She'd been a willing pussy, and after he'd had her, he'd pretty much forgotten about her.

The problem was, her words still lingered. Not every woman liked having a man leave instructions for them, or pick out their clothes, or being the man of the house. There was no other way he could be. He'd always been the one in control.

"What did you expect me to do?" she asked.

"I don't know what I expected you to do. It doesn't really matter either."

"It clearly does."

Looking past her shoulder, he tried to get his thoughts into some kind of focus, but nothing was happening.

"I didn't expect you to simply wear the clothes, or go and make breakfast."

"You were testing me?"

"Yes."

Her smile surprised him. How was it that Maria, his little virgin, was always surprising him?

"I passed your test," she said.

"Yes."

She leaned in close, cupping his cheek. "You're going to have to realize really quickly that I'm full of surprises." She pressed a kiss to his lips. "I don't have any plans after our four weeks. I can tell you what I hope, but again, hoping is not really planning."

"Then tell me your hopes."

He picked up the basket, and they started walking again. "I'm hoping we find something here that we've both been hunting for. I want to be with a man I love, respect, and trust. I'm not going to be some doormat who'll wait at home for her man. It's not what I want. I want to provide a home for the both of us. I want to be doing our shopping, the cleaning, the cooking, and organizing special dates. When we have kids, I want you to know that I can handle whatever life throws at us. I also want to be the wife that you need with the Trojans."

Daisy understood what she meant. He wasn't looking for some doormat who'd do what he wanted. Maria was a strong mind, a strong woman, who merely wanted to put her trust into a man who'd take care of her.

"Do you think you could handle the club life?"

"An old lady club life?"

"Yes." There would be no room for anyone else. The thought of another man touching her filled him with a lot of anger. Maria belonged to him, and he wasn't having anyone tell him differently.

"I do. I like the old ladies. Sheila is also a sweetheart." Sheila was Russ's old lady and was Holly's mother.

There was a lot of history at the club. He liked Sheila. She was a good woman, and one Russ had nearly lost.

"What do you think of Knuckles?" Maria asked, surprising him with the change of subject.

"Why are you talking about Knuckles?" Jealousy struck him hard, and unexpectedly. He never thought he'd feel jealous of another brother, but that was exactly what he was thinking and feeling. The feeling swirled in the pit of his stomach, and he couldn't stop it.

"I've seen the way he watches Beth."

As quickly as the jealousy struck, it started to fizzle out.

"Knuckles won't touch Beth."

"I'm not saying she's in danger. He looks at her, and sees her, you know? Beth's never had that. I've never seen a guy really look at a woman, and see her for her true self. It's beautiful to see."

I look at you like that.

Get a grip, Daisy.

There was no one else out there for him but the woman beside him. Great, he'd been with her less than forty-eight hours, and already he was losing his mind. They continued walking down the long dirt path. It was warm, and the long branches with thick leaves gave them enough cover.

Just up ahead he saw Lucinda and Phil with several people coming up the path. Squeezing Maria's hand, he headed toward them. It had been too long since he'd seen the happy couple.

"Daisy," Phil said, speaking up first. Lucinda had been talking to a woman behind her, and turned toward him.

He shook hands with Phil and laughed as Lucinda hugged him. "How was the cabin? I worked my ass off to make it livable again."

"It's great. I want you to meet someone." Tugging Maria in front of him, he wrapped an arm around her waist, and smiled across her shoulder. "This was the special woman I was talking about."

"Daisy?"

He frowned, looking past Lucinda to the woman that had spoken, and he froze up as he spotted his ex, Laura. What the fuck was she doing here?

She had interrupted the introduction, and now he was shocked to have seen her. Daisy hadn't seen Laura since she'd stormed out of his apartment years ago. What the fuck was she doing here now?

"Do you two know each other?" Lucinda asked.

"Yes," Daisy said.

Maria tensed in his arms.

Drawing his attention away from the woman, he smiled at Lucinda and Phil. "I wanted you two to meet my woman, Maria."

"It's a pleasure to meet you," Maria said. "You did an amazing job with his cabin."

"I'm afraid we can't stop and talk. We've got to keep on schedule. We'd love to have you over for dinner," Phil said.

"I'll call and we can arrange it."

Phil had spotted the tension, and was now moving the problem out of his way. Daisy liked Phil and Lucinda.

Laura made no attempt to talk to him, and he was thankful. He didn't want to talk to that woman, or have her ruin his time with Maria.

Picking up the picnic basket, they kept on moving, and it was only a matter of time before Maria asked questions.

"You do know I saw all of that, right? I saw your reaction, and what happened."

He sighed. "I've got nothing to hide."

"Who was the woman that recognized you?"

Did he detect a hint of jealousy in her voice?

He was so fucking happy about that. She didn't have a single thing to jealous about, but he wasn't about to complain if that was exactly what she thought.

****

Who was that woman?

Why did Daisy tense up?

Maria couldn't stop the questions swirling around in her head, driving her crazy. They made their way further down the path that Lucinda and Phil had come up. She heard the subtle sound of rushing water, and Daisy led them off the path, down a slight embankment.

He hadn't answered her question, and she didn't know if she should be pissed off with that.

Suddenly he stopped. "I want you to stand here. Don't move."

Daisy left her alone, and Maria stood in her space, watching him disappear. She closed her eyes and basked in the sounds of nature, the chirping of birds, the water, the air as it rustled the leaves on the trees. Each sound relaxed and calmed her. She loved it.

Seconds passed, and when she was about to go and follow Daisy, he appeared once again, stepping behind her.

"I want you to trust me." He covered her eyes with his hands, and she released a sigh. She followed his movements, as he started her walking.

Placing her hands over his, they walked past a bush that was really close as the scent invaded her senses.

They walked for a few more steps, and then Daisy stopped.

"The woman who recognized me was Laura. She's the woman who walked out on me for picking out her clothes. I didn't expect her to be here. I haven't seen her in years. The last time I saw her, she was packing her shit up and leaving." He kissed her neck. "You've got nothing to be worried about. Seeing her, it was a shock, but she's not the woman I want." He released her eyes, and she still had them closed. "Open your eyes."

She opened her eyes and gasped.

Daisy had found a hidden oasis, and it really was a thing of beauty. She'd never seen anything so beautiful in all of her life. There was a slight waterfall up ahead that expanded out into a thick river. It was beautiful, and she was in awe of what was in front of her.

Flowers seemed brighter, and through the leaves of the trees, sunshine filtered down, lighting everything up.

"Wow."

"Yes, wow." He moved toward a thin blanket, and she couldn't help but be touched. Daisy had set up their picnic. Plates were on the blanket, drinks, and food was laid out. "Are you hungry?"

"I didn't think I was." She took a seat opposite him, and looked around. Staring across the embankment, her mouth literally fell open as she spotted a doe eating some grass. "This is beautiful."

"You've got to be quiet or she'll run."

The doe was so beautiful, and Maria couldn't believe she'd never seen one before in her life. Sure, she'd seen them in books, and in movies, but this was real life. She was staring across the large river.

"Isn't she afraid?" Maria asked.

"Probably. We're not going to hurt her. Maybe she knows we're not a threat."

Daisy poured them both a drink, and handed one to her. She took a drink of the strawberry and kiwi water, enjoying the fresh taste as it exploded on her tongue.

"You didn't love Laura?"

"I couldn't stand the bitch. She was good for one thing."

"She still made you doubt yourself as a person." Maria averted her gaze, and focused on him in front of her. "Admit it, your little test this morning was because of that woman."

"Yes, it was."

"Why?"

"Let's just say that even a man like me has insecurities."

"It seemed off for you to admit it."

He laughed. "I'm struggling to evolve."

Sipping her drink, she looked toward the doe. Sadness gripped her as the animal had wandered off. Life would be so much easier if she was a doe.

"I think my parents are in a Dominant and submissive relationship," she said, spilling out the words.

"What makes you think that?"

"The way they are with each other. Over the years I've noticed subtle differences between my parents and yours. Also, I went into my mother's jewelry box when she was out with my father, and I noticed on one of the bracelets she wore it read, 'Property of Master'." After she had seen that one item, she'd gone through everything, and then like a crazy person, she'd watched her parents.

"What do you think?"

"It makes sense. I love my parents. They're totally in love with each other. I was the mistake. They can't have their real relationship with me living with them."

Daisy gripped the back of her neck and pulled her toward him. He slammed his lips against hers, and she melted.

"We won't be like that," he said, breaking away from the kiss.

"I know. You're not a Dominant." She cupped his cheek. "You shouldn't let her control you, Daisy. Be who you're meant to be."

"Then come here." He patted the blanket beside her.

Without hesitation she moved over the blanket until she settled beside him.

"Lie down."

"You're always asking me to do that." Settling down on the blanket beside him, she placed her hands on her stomach. "What else would you like?"

"Lift your hands above your head, and don't move."

She took a deep breath, and lifted her hands above her head, aware of how the action pressed her tits up.

Daisy reached over her, starting at her wrist, and slid the tips of his fingers down one arm. He paused at the top of her chest. He turned her head so that she stared up at him.

"Your body drives me crazy."

"You don't think I'm too big?"

"No. You're perfect. I love how big your tits are, and the way your nipples are always hard for me."

The bra he'd picked for her was lace, so it didn't offer much protection against his gaze.

"I've been with slender women, Maria, and they don't hold anything to you. You're woman all over." His fingers moved down, gliding straight across her nipple, down to the bottom of her tank top. He lifted it up so that it was bunched up underneath her chin. "Keep those hands above your head. I'm going to have a little play." He cupped her breast, and in the next second tugged down the cup of her bra to rest underneath her tit. "So responsive." Daisy did the same to the next cup, exposing both of her tits and making it so the bra pushed her tits up in an offering.

He pinched one nipple, then the other. Crying out, Maria arched up unable to control the shock of pleasure his touch created.

"There is no other kind of woman out there for me but you. I don't give a shit about the Lauras of this world, and even if she came to me naked, offering me everything, you're the only one I want. She can't give me you, only you can."

That had to be the nicest, sweetest thing that anyone had ever said to her. She was totally shocked by the sincerity in his voice.

"I've always watched you, Maria, even when you thought I wasn't. It wasn't in a creepy way. I had to protect you, and make sure you were safe. I remember being there when you first learned to ride a bike. You couldn't trust anyone, not my dad or your own. There was no one you'd trust, and then both of our parents went to have a drink. It was just you, me, and Beth. I moved behind you, and said, let's get this going. You gripped the handlebars so tightly, but you allowed me to stand behind you, and start the bike."

Tears filled her eyes at the memory. It was so clear in her mind that it was like she was living it. Her father had the afternoon off work, and instead of taking her mother out to dinner, he'd come to help her.

She'd felt like such a disappointment to him as she couldn't trust him to not let her fall. Instead, the time had passed with her father moving her across the grass toward Daisy's father. Maria had been aware of Daisy watching the whole time. He'd been to visit his family on one of his rare occasions home. She'd been nine, and he'd been nineteen, and already part of the Trojans. His family hadn't liked him coming around, but Daisy wasn't the kind of man to not do something because someone else didn't like it. He'd visited Beth, and his home, every chance he got.

"I pushed the bike, and I took a handful of steps, and when I told you to not panic, and start pedaling, you did it. You kept on pedaling. For ten minutes that's what we did, and when your father came back, he closed down, and went back home," Daisy said. "I wanted to beat the shit out of the fucker for that."

"Really?"

"Yes. He didn't need to throw a tantrum like that. Your father, your parents, they do love you, Maria."

He stroked over her nipples, paying careful attention to each before moving down her stomach to the button that held up her shorts. Daisy flicked it open, and slid his hand inside.

She took a deep breath, waiting for him to take it just that little bit further.

Chapter Seven

Daisy slid his hand inside her shorts, touching the flesh of her sex. She was so slick and beautiful. He stroked her clit, watching as she bit her lip, fighting the pleasure. Thinking about their past together, he recalled many times where he'd gotten angry with her father. He'd even gone to see Maria's father to let him know what he was doing to his daughter. Daisy cared about Maria even then. He'd seen how hungry she was for affection, and had tried to steer his family toward her.

They were not happy with him or his decision to be part of an MC, but that didn't mean they couldn't extend their love toward Maria. He wanted her, and cared for her. She'd always brought out this protective instinct inside him.

"This pussy belongs to me, baby." He cupped her pussy, tempted to slide his finger inside her.

No, you'll claim her in a bed, and make her yours.

Daisy had a lot of plans for his woman, and he wasn't going to mess it up by rushing their time together. Leaning down, he claimed her lips, sliding his tongue into her mouth, deepening the kiss.

She whimpered and started to thrust her pussy onto his fingers. Working her clit, Daisy took his time, and throughout awakening her body, he kept on kissing her. This wasn't about him, but about Maria. He wanted her to learn to trust him, and for her realize that he wasn't going to force her to take him.

Maria wiggled on his finger, and he teased her clit, quickening his strokes then slowing them down. She tried to pull her lips away from him, and Daisy wouldn't break away from the kiss.

Her breathing increased, and she started to pant. His woman was so close to exploding, and he was more than happy to swallow her cries. Daisy brought her to orgasm, prolonging her pleasure for as long as he could before finally pulling away.

Staring into her eyes, he licked his fingers, tasting her cream.

Her cheeks heated, and he chuckled. "You're going to have to get used to me doing that."

"I don't know if I can."

"Even if you don't, I love seeing you blush." He pressed a quick kiss to her nose. "Now, where were we?"

"I can't think." She placed her hands against her heated cheeks.

"Good. You're not supposed to think." He took hold of her hands, and locked their fingers together. "Now, talk to me, Maria. What do you want to do with your life? Don't hold anything back."

She licked her lips, and he couldn't resist capturing them for another kiss.

"Don't hold back on me, Maria." He rested his head on his hand, smiling down at her.

"What I want?"

"What you want from life."

"Like what?"

"Okay, I want a woman who can accept me being the man of the house. I'll provide for her, take care of her, love her, protect her, and I'll be the one wearing the pants." He looked down her body. "I'll like you in jeans every now and again, but not all the time. You'll support me, and I'll support you."

"What you're telling me isn't scaring me, Daisy."

"Some women want to go out and earn a living. I respect that. Mary and Holly, they have their commitments with work. Leanna is rich, and Zoe is finishing up college. I want to be your world, Maria. Me, and the kids we have. Can you handle that?"

They had to be completely honest with each other, and put their needs out there for the other to understand how far this was going to go.

"You want kids?"

"Yes."

"I don't know what I want from my future. I want kids, and I guess I want to finish college. I don't want to be sitting around all day waiting for you, but could I help Mary and Holly? Do you think they'd allow me to help them? I couldn't do nothing all day."

Daisy laughed. "You'd be busy with club business, baby. We own several businesses around town, but not just that, we also own a mechanics shop where you can help. You'll be mine, though, completely."

"Yours?"

"Yes. No other man, no other women. You'll be mine, my woman to love, to fuck, and to claim." Daisy cupped her cheek and stroked his thumb across her bottom lip. "Can you handle that?"

"When you used to visit Beth after you joined the MC, I always made sure that I could sleep over at her house. You're the only guy that I know who intrigued me, and made me want to be with someone."

"I thought you hated me."

"I didn't hate you. I was scared you'd laugh at me, see me as nothing more than a schoolgirl who had a crush. It was embarrassing. Every time Beth talked about you, I couldn't help but listen. I'd wait to hear your bike, and I made sure I had to see Beth. You didn't always announce your visits to your parents."

He'd had no idea.

Daisy had thought she hated him and what he stood for.

She placed her hand over the patch of his leather jacket. "This is who you are. I did some research, and I found that I loved what you were part of. Don't get me wrong, the MC life is scary to me. You could go to jail, and do some hard time, but I wanted to be part of your world. To know the kind of freedom you live."

"What do you mean?" he asked.

He'd known Maria's parents weren't exactly giving in many areas of their lives. Daisy hadn't been around all the time, but he'd witnessed Maria's sadness when she looked at her parents. They always had time for each other, yet they overlooked her. It was because of her parents that he'd made a vow to always make sure his kids knew he loved them, and to show them affection.

You also made yourself a promise that you would take care of Maria.

Daisy had wanted her for so long, and now she was in his arms. He wasn't going to let her go.

"You never cared about what others thought of you. You were happy with yourself, and you never waited for anyone to take care of you." Her smile was breathtaking. "When I saw you, I knew I wanted to be like you. Well, not like you, but not care what my parents thought, or my teachers. The only person who ever enjoyed my company was Beth. She's been my rock for all my life."

He didn't like the sadness that suddenly clouded her eyes.

"You don't just have Beth. You've got me, and I'm not going to let you go."

"I was never good enough for them, Daisy. It didn't matter how many good grades I got, or how much I fought to make them proud. Nothing was ever good enough. I was always too needy, in the way, not doing enough sports, eating all the time. I was just never, ever good enough."

"You're good enough for me, and if they can't see that, fuck 'em. You're perfect, and don't let anyone in this miserable world tell you otherwise. That's another thing I want you to do if we make this official," he said.

"What?"

"Stop listening to everything else, and everyone else. I'm the one that is important, me, not them."

He claimed her lips, and moved his body over hers. Taking hold of her hands, he placed them above her head. "Who matters?" he asked.

"You do."

"Who counts?"

"You do."

"Remember that, baby."

****

Beth stood at the kitchen window and stared out across the backyard of the clubhouse. Daisy and Maria had been gone a full day. It was nighttime, and she had yet to hear from him. She wasn't nervous about being alone in the clubhouse, but without Maria, she didn't know what to do.

Maria took her out shopping. Her friend made her cook, eat, and actually do something with her life. The only thing she'd done so far was inform her parents that she was sticking around. They hadn't argued, but she wasn't an idiot. The moment she got off the phone, she just bet that her father was on the phone to her brother.

She hated this feeling of emptiness, of not belonging. Staring out at the members partying in the yard, she really wished she could be part of it all. The women were so confident as they got naked around the men. She smiled as she watched Landon feeling up one of the club whores, whom she believed was called Lori. Beth had seen her sniffing around Daisy to no avail. Her brother had been in love with Maria for a long time. He simply didn't know it yet.

"What are you doing in here alone?" Knuckles asked, coming to stand behind her. She couldn't help closing her eyes from his closeness. What was it about this man that didn't have her running scared?

His very presence comforted her and chased away the demons that held her captive.

"I'm not exactly a party girl." She nodded outside. "I wouldn't fit in."

"There's more ways to have fun. Come on." He took her hand and started to make his way out of the kitchen.

"Wait, what are you doing?" Beth asked.

No one was around, and when he made his way back toward his bedroom, she started to panic and pull away from him.

"Let me go! Please, let me go!"

Knuckles didn't stop until he got to his bedroom door. She knew it was his door as she'd seen him come in and out of it enough times. He released her, and she sagged against the wall, taking deep breaths.

He cupped her face. This time she didn't fight him, caught in his gaze.

"I will never ever hurt you, Beth."

"What?"

"You're panicking, and I see the terror in your eyes. Don't be afraid. You're safe with me. I'll never take what is not offered. Whoever hurt you, his days are numbered."

"No one hu—"

"Don't even think of fucking lying to me. I'm not a stupid idiot. I know something happened to you, something bad, and I'm not going to pretend it didn't. I'm also not going to force you to tell me. When you're ready, you'll tell me. The day that happens, whoever put his filthy hands on you, he's dead."

She should be nervous by his threat.

She wasn't.

Beth wanted Benedict dead.

Could she have his death on her conscience?

Knuckles stroked a finger across her cheek, tucking some hair behind her ear. "You're safe with me, Beth." He opened his door, and entered. She took several deep breaths before moving toward his doorway. Beth didn't know what she expected, but it wasn't him sitting on a sofa at the end of his bed, holding a remote control. "Want to play?"

"Huh?"

"Like I said, there's more ways to have fun. I find playing relaxing, and it's fun." He leaned over the sofa, and held a bag of cheesy chips. "I've also got snacks. What do you say?"

"This is it?"

"Close the door," he said as she entered his room.

She turned to shut the door before facing him again. "This is it?"

"What else did you think I had in mind?"

"I don't know ... sex?"

Knuckles laughed. "As much as I'd love to fuck you, Beth, you're not ready. We'll get to that soon enough. You know it's there. Now, do you want to play?"

Taking a seat beside him, she stared at the computer game, which looked like some kind of fighting game. She didn't recognize it, but when Knuckles handed her the remote, she started to play.

"Thank you," she said, once several seconds had gone by.

"Why?"

"You're not rushing me, or forcing me."

"Time will come for that, baby. Right now, try and kick my ass."

She started to giggle as they attacked each other on the screen.

****

"You want us to do what?" Pie asked from his position around the church table.

Duke stared around at his brothers, the men he'd willingly die for, and who he trusted with his woman, Holly. "Matthew's coming on as a Prospect. I want you to treat him worse than a Prospect."

He saw all the men glancing at each other. Raoul and Landon were smiling as if he was talking crazy. Pike and Crazy were the only two taking it seriously. Chip, Knuckles, Floss, Brass, Smash, and several others were not taking him seriously. He'd called a church meeting early in the morning as he wanted this shit dealt with.

"You mean you've woke me up to tell me your son is going to be a Prospect?" Daisy asked. They had put him on speaker so they could all hear.

"We can't treat Matthew any differently than anyone else. That's not how our deal works," Knuckles said. "He gets given the same tests as everyone else."

Duke ran fingers through his hair, and let out a sigh. "I know what you're saying, Knuckles, I really do, but we test Prospects over time. Matthew is still in high school. I'm asking as a personal favor to me. Matthew is not ready to take on the Trojans MC. He's also not ready for the fact his dick gets hard, and he's fucking girls left, right, and center. What I want is for him to wake the fuck up. He's a man, and he's not behaving like one. He figures because he's getting his dick wet, it makes him a man." He now had all of their attention, and they were all taking him seriously.

Crazy was the first to speak up. "You want to give him a crash course in being a man?"

"Yes. He doesn't get any club pussy, and he doesn't get any special treatment. He's not my son."

"What does Holly know about this?" Russ, her father, asked.

"She knows I'm going to be putting some pressure on my boy. Don't get me wrong, this is going to hurt, but I need him to see his options here."

"I've spoken to Holly. She wants Matthew to go to college," Pike said.

"Wouldn't you?" Duke asked.

"What happens if he passes?" Raoul asked.

Duke knew there was a risk of Matthew being able to handle what the club threw at him. What he hoped was for his son to have a wakeup call. "Matthew has grown up within this club. You've always had his back, and he figures it's going to be an easy change from kid to patched in member. Everyone has to go through Prospecting. It's a rite of passage into the club for everyone."

"He's right. If Holly had been a boy, she'd have had to go through being a Prospect, and I'd expect you all to treat her like any other Prospect."

"Well, Holly's not a guy, and never wanted to be part of the club." His woman hadn't hated the club life, but she'd never wanted to be an old lady. Duke had soon changed her mind about that. She still didn't like the thought of Matthew going through the life, but he'd asked her to trust him about this.

Matthew was a smart boy, and he'd see that college was the right way. There would always be a spot here for him, just not right now.

"If he cries, you're not going to kick our ass, right?" Knuckles asked.

"He's only seventeen. He doesn't get to see the fun stuff, and tell the club whores to ignore him like any other Prospect. Matthew gets the cleaning shit, the driving, and getting everything that Prospects hate about the club."

Pike chuckled. "This is going to be fun."

Duke hoped so, and he hoped Matthew grew from the experience. It wouldn't be long before he was eighteen, and he could make the decisions himself. Until that day came, Duke was the one in charge, and his kid would do what was right.

Dropping the gavel, he ended the call with Daisy, and watched his men file out of the room. Russ stayed behind just like he knew Russ would.

"You all right?" Russ asked.

They were alone, and Duke sagged in his chair.

"Yes, no, and every fucking thing in between. Kids were not supposed to be easy."

Russ burst out laughing. "You've got two boys. One of which is old enough to wipe his own ass, and you're thinking it's hard? Try having a girl."

Duke tensed up, looking toward his father-in-law. "Girls are easy?"

Another laugh came from Russ. "No, girls appear easy. They're fucking hard work, Duke. Holly, she was always a sweet child, and she loved the club. Then she grew up, and her troubles started. I can tell you the first time she received her menstrual cycle, if it hadn't been for Sheila I'd have had a breakdown. Not only was my baby growing up, I knew boys were going to notice that shit, too. The worst thing in the world is having a daughter, and knowing there were guys like yourself growing up. It makes you realize what an asshole you'd been."

"Fuck!" Duke didn't even want to think of having a girl. "Pike's got a girl."

"I know, and he doesn't have a clue what is coming to him. Makes you feel sorry for the bastard, a little."

Duke smiled. "Seriously, Russ, do you think I'm doing the right thing?"

Russ sighed. "Matthew's a good kid, and like all good kids, they need a little guidance. You're providing him that. Don't let the shit go too far, and make sure he can come to you. You'll be fine."

"He thinks the girls are going to fuck him."

"Then he's going to get a fucking wakeup call." Russ stood. "Trust your gut, Duke. It hasn't done you wrong so far."

Nodding, he watched his father-in-law leave the church. He wasn't surprised when Holly entered the room with Drake on her hip.

"They're in?"

"They're in, and you've got to trust me."

"I do trust you. I just hate that it has to happen."

"I know." He got to his feet, and took Drake from her. Wrapping an arm around her waist, he tugged her close, rubbing his nose against hers. "I never want to have girls."

"Then you better tell your little swimmers to be good. I can't control what we have."

She pressed her lips against his, and all of his concerns evaporated with her in his arms.

He really did love this woman.

Chapter Eight

One week later

Maria was losing her mind with all the pleasure Daisy was wreaking on her body. He wasn't doing it right now, but it had been one long week of pleasure beneath his hands.

You're still a virgin.

Yes, one week in Daisy's bed, in his arms for the past twenty-four hours, over the last seven days, and she was still a virgin. It had to be some kind of record with this guy. She'd known Daisy a long time, and he was a highly sexed man. Even now, they were playing with each other, bringing each other to orgasm multiple times a day.

She wanted sex, craved sex, needed sex, and that was just it—he wasn't giving it.

He was already awake this morning, and she saw the pastel blue summer dress with a lacy white bra. She loved the way he was always picking out her clothes.

Biting her lip, she climbed out of bed, and looked down at her body.

"Still a virgin!"

Her breasts were a little sore and tender from Daisy's lips and hands. Moving toward the mirror, she stared at her reflection, and wondered what she was going to do with him.

"I want to have sex." Shaking her head, she reached for her bra and started putting it on. Next, she went for the dress. Daisy never allowed her to wear panties, and she was nervous. Her menstrual cycle would be starting in two weeks. Did he know women went through that?

Leaving the bedroom, she walked down the corridor, and paused when she saw Daisy speaking to Lucinda and Phil. They were in the sitting room of their cabin, and she forced a smile to her lips.

Lucinda noticed her first.

"Good morning," Lucinda said.

Daisy turned toward her, and he smiled. "Hey, baby. I was just going to come and wake you up."

He stood and moved toward her side, wrapping an arm around her waist.

Still not having sex with me.

Great, she was becoming obsessed with sex, and that was never a good thing.

"We dropped in without an invitation. I'm surprised Daisy's allowing us to keep living," Phil said, laughing.

"Well, you two can get away with it." Daisy stroked her hip, and her body once again came alive. She couldn't even talk to Beth about this. It would be too creepy talking to Daisy's sister in the hope of finding out how to have sex with him. "Come on."

He eased her down to sit beside him, and she took a deep breath, smiling at the sweet couple.

"So, Lucinda and I were extending an invitation to you to come eat dinner. Most of the tours have been done for the summer, and we're winding down. We're thinking a small barbeque, some music. What do you say?" Phil asked.

"I'd love to. Maria and I will be here for another couple of weeks, and then we'll be heading back to Vale Valley." Daisy pressed a kiss to her head.

Still not had sex, buddy.

He was treating her—she didn't even know how he was treating her, only that he was not having sex with her.

"That reminds me. I just want to warn you that Laura has been asking after you."

"What?" Daisy asked, tensing up.

Maria wasn't too happy about it either. Laura, even though he didn't love her, had been the first woman he'd been natural with. That woman had made him try to stop his own needs, and that pissed her off.

"What has she been asking?"

Lucinda looked at Phil. "You may as well tell him."

"She wants to know who you're here with, and if you're, erm, married? Just personal stuff."

"What have you said?" Daisy asked.

"We don't divulge personal information about our guests. You own this cabin, but you're a personal friend, Daisy. We wouldn't let anything personal go. I can promise you that."

He nodded. "Thank you. I appreciate that."

Phil cleared his throat. "We better go."

"Yes. I'm sorry for invading your morning." Lucina and Phil stood, and she stood beside Daisy's side.

You're making plans with Daisy.

Long term plans.

No sex.

Sex doesn't matter.

She hated the insecurity that was filling her. It sucked.

"What is it?" he asked.

Phil and Lucinda were walking away, and Maria shook her head.

"Nothing."

"Do you not want to go to their place for dinner?"

"I'm looking forward to going to dinner with them." She moved toward the kitchen, but Daisy stopped her, grabbing her hand, and pulling her toward him.

"What is it? Don't lie to me."

She stared into his eyes.

No sex.

No sex.

No sex.

It didn't have to mean something, but it was going around and around in her head, and it was driving her crazy. She wasn't used to being like this, and she hated it.

"It's nothing. I guess I don't like Laura asking questions about you. Can I, erm, can I call Beth?" she asked.

"Sure."

He pulled his cell phone out of his pocket and handed it to her. "It means nothing."

"Huh?"

"Laura. She means nothing to me, and the only person I care about is you. It's never going to change."

She nodded. "I know. Do you want me to do breakfast?"

He tilted his head, looking at her. "I'll fix breakfast this morning. Tell Beth I miss her." He stepped close to her, cupping her cheek, and pressing a kiss to her temple.

No sex.

Opening the door to the cabin, she stepped out and dialed Beth's number. It rang several times, and when a masculine voiced answered, Maria frowned.

"Who is it?" the guy said.

"Erm, who are you? This is Beth's phone."

"Shit, two seconds." She heard scuffling, and then Beth's name. "Someone's on the phone."

"What?" Beth asked.

Shit, what the hell was Beth doing in bed with someone? What was going on?

"Hello," Beth said.

"Who the hell is that?" Maria asked.

"Maria?"

"Yeah, you better be damned happy it was me, otherwise Daisy would be losing it right now." She looked through the window and saw Daisy staring at a packet. That man clearly didn't know how to cook.

"Shit!" More noise came from Beth's end, and Maria winced, moving out of the way of the window so Daisy couldn't see her. "Right, I'm alone. Morning, Maria."

"Oh no, oh hell no. You don't get to do that shit to me, and then pretend that I'm not going to ask questions. Who was the man in your bed, and why are you acting all funny?" she asked.

Beth sighed. "I was with Knuckles."

"You're having sex with Knuckles?"

"No, I'm not having sex with Knuckles. We were playing a video game like we've been doing for the past couple of days, and time got away from me. That's all."

"That's all?"

"Yes. Nothing has happened. Not like I'm guessing you're getting it on with my brother, and I have to say that I'm totally grossed out right now. Like, seriously sick to the stomach just thinking about you two together. I'm happy for you though."

"That's was a strange way of putting it."

"Daisy is my brother, which equals ew. You're my best friend, and yeah, I'm happy for you."

"Well, you can be rest assured that you don't have to worry about Daisy and me doing the ew."

"What?"

"I'm still a virgin. A complete and total virgin. My hymen is still intact, and at this right, it's going to get calcified." She was never going to have sex, and playing with Daisy wasn't helping. He was only increasing her need to be with him. They had taken the time to explore each other, and she'd sucked his cock, and he'd licked her pussy. Together they had many hours worth of play, and still, it hadn't changed anything. Maria wanted Daisy, she craved him, and it was driving her crazy being close to him, and not being with him.

"I don't think your hymen can get calcified," Beth said, laughing.

"Stop laughing at me, okay? Have you known Daisy to take his time?"

"You do realize you're asking me how often Daisy sleeps with someone?"

"Yes. This is not normal."

"Have you ever considered the fact that Daisy's respecting you?" Beth asked.

"Ugh, you're not going to help me. So, why don't we start talking about something else? Like, what is going on with you and Knuckles?"

"Nothing is going on with me and Knuckles. We're friends, and that's all."

"Do you want something to be going on with him?" Maria asked. She was trying to be a good friend, right?

"I'm not looking for something more. Knuckles knows this."

"You hope he knows this."

"I'm not going to tell him about what happened. He'd kill him."

"Benedict needs to die," Maria said.

"I'm not liking this phone call anymore."

"You don't like anything anymore."

Beth blew a raspberry, and Maria couldn't help but laugh.

"You know, you could just ask him."

"What?" Maria asked.

"Ask Daisy. Tell that you want to have sex, and I'm sure he'll be more than happy to oblige you. I can't even believe I'm saying this to you."

"I know. It's crazy, right?" Maria asked. "We're going out tonight to a party. Hey, have you ever heard of a woman called Laura? She's Daisy's ex."

"I recall him dating someone called Laura, but that was about it. I didn't spend all that much time around his girlfriends. Why?"

"She's here, and asking stuff about Daisy. I want to claw her eyes out."

"Are you worried about the competition?" Beth asked.

"No, yes, I don't know. He says it's over, but it had been a week since he last saw her, and we've not had any sex. We've done a lot more stuff, and he does this thing with his tongue—"

"Ew, brother remember. I don't need to know what trick he does with his tongue or anything like that."

Maria laughed. "Oops, sorry."

"Look, Daisy's not like anyone I know. He's my brother, and he cares about you, Maria. He always asked after you when he called, and wanted to make sure you were okay. That has to count for something, right? Talk to him, trust him, and have some fun."

"I'm having fun. We've been talking about the future, and what we want from life."

"I'd love to have you as my sister. You've always been my sister, and you and Daisy were meant to be together."

"Thank you," Maria said.

"I'm going to go and hunt for breakfast."

"Be careful with Knuckles."

"There's nothing going on. He's actually a really nice guy, and it's not just because of me being related to Daisy. I like him, Maria."

"You deserve to be happy. Just be warned, Daisy's not going to like it."

****

Daisy looked out of Phil and Lucinda's main garden that overlooked the entire vacation land. He saw his own cabin that was hidden mostly by trees, but he made it out. Phil would have had a field day if he'd been looking at his cabin.

"So, are you going to marry this one?" Phil asked, coming to stand beside him. They both held a bottle of beer, and he glanced toward the house to see Lucinda and Maria talking.

"I'm thinking about it."

"I see the look in your eye. It's exactly the same one I feel every time I look at Lucinda." Phil followed his gaze. "I love my wife, and she was more than happy to help me set up this crazy dream."

"This was always your dream?"

"Yes. Lucinda worked in the city as a divorce attorney, and I was the CEO of a big ass company. I wasn't happy, she wasn't happy. Neither of us were happy, and we came to this exclusive nature resort as a way to try rekindle our love. The older couple was struggling to keep with the maintenance of this place. Lucinda and I were happy for once, and neither of us wanted to leave. We bought this place from them, and the rest is history."

Daisy watched Maria as she laughed along with Lucinda over something.

"You love her?" Phil asked.

"Yes." He spoke the word without hesitation, and something calmed inside him. Daisy was in love with Maria, and had always been in love with her.

You've not had sex with her yet.

He'd not wanted to risk hurting her. What if he wasn't gentle enough with her? What if he hurt her, and she never wanted him?

For the first time in his life, he was actually afraid of losing her, and that didn't sit well with him. He wanted her badly, and that wasn't all. Daisy wanted her as his old lady, the love of his life, and the mother of his child.

"It makes everything easier if you're more than willing to admit how you feel."

"Is that what happened with Lucinda?"

"Yes. I would die for that woman."

Daisy would do the same for his own woman.

"What are you two lovebirds talking about?" Lucinda asked, coming out of the kitchen.

"Women, love, and all in between." Phil moved toward Lucinda's side, pulling her in tight against him.

"You were talking about love?" Maria asked.

He wrapped his arm around her waist and pulled her in close. "Yeah, what were you two talking about?"

"She was telling me about Laura."

"You don't have to worry about her, baby. There's no comparison, babe." He tugged her in front of him, and rubbed his cock against her ass. "That's what you do to me."

"Yeah right!"

He heard the sarcasm in her voice. "Excuse me?"

"Nothing."

Turning her to face him, he tilted her head back to stare into her eyes. "There's clearly something wrong with you."

"You're aroused, but I bet any woman could take care of your problem. It's not just me, and you and I know it."

Okay, she had just confused him.

"I don't follow. You're the woman I've been talking about sharing my life with, and you're telling me that you don't think I want you."

She looked toward Lucinda and Phil before continuing. The couple was a little ways from them, offering some privacy. "We've not had sex, Daisy. You don't want me, and that's fine. Instead of stringing me along, just tell me you don't want anything to do with me, and I'll stop making a fool of myself."

He took hold of her hand and placed it over his cock. "I want you, and I want to fuck you for a long time. I've been waiting so that you'd feel more comfortable around me. This isn't about me, babe. This is about you."

"Me? How is it about me?"

"You're a virgin, and I'm going to be your first time. Do you think I'm not aware of how painful it can be for you, or what I could do to hurt you? I'm taking my time with you."

"What?" she asked, looking confused.

"You're going to be the first woman I've been with who is a virgin. I've never claimed a woman's cherry before, and never wanted to. When we have sex, I want you to be ready."

"I am ready."

"Maria?"

"No, I'm ready, and this is about me. I'm more than ready to be yours, Daisy. This is what our time was about, right? Being away from the club, and unable to run from each other. One week has gone, and I've opened up to you, and you've yet to take things to the next level."

Daisy cupped her cheek. "Let's enjoy some food with our friends, and then we'll see what happens later tonight."

"Are you two lovebirds done talking?" Phil asked.

They gathered around the barbeque, and Daisy kept his hand on Maria's waist, not wanting to let her go. He loved this woman, and he wouldn't let anything happen to her. As the evening wore on he saw that both Lucinda and Phil liked her, and he loved that. They ate good food, drank a couple of beers, and talked about everything. Lucinda and Maria had a lot in common, and they had a love of nature. She also talked extensively to Phil about the latest television series.

He actually had a lot of fun.

By ten at night, he was more than ready to take his woman home, and he let his friends know it with a single look.

Taking hold of her hand, they walked all the way back to their cabin. The stars were aglow in the night sky, and she rested her head against his shoulder.

"I loved tonight," Maria said.

"Me too. Lucinda and Phil really do like you."

"I like them, too. I was thinking we could come here regularly to get away from it all."

"I like that idea. I want to bring you here so I can keep you naked all the time."

She chuckled. "You do like me naked."

"Daisy? Is that you?"

Maria tensed in his arms, and Daisy grew angry that the woman was being pretty persistent.

Holding onto his woman, he turned to face Laura. "What do you want?"

Laura's gaze wandered over Maria, and he held her just a little tighter.

"Is she with you?"

"Yes. Maria, I'd like you to meet Laura. Laura, this is my old lady, Maria."

"Old lady? That's club speech."

"I belong to him," Maria said. "In the eyes of the club I'm as good as married to him."

That's right, my little firecracker.
You belong to me, and I love you.

"Daisy and I go way back," Laura said.

"Actually, Maria and I go way back." He wasn't about to let Laura think she had a spot in his life when it wasn't true. "What do you want?"

"I was wondering if you'd like to get a drink and catch up."

"I saw you here with your husband. Why on earth would you want to catch up with me? We don't have anything to talk about."

Laura gave him a wicked smile and stepped close. She was about to place her finger against his chest, and Maria shocked him. Maria grabbed Laura's hand tightly.

"You've got nothing to talk about with my man, Laura."

"You don't know Daisy at all, do you? He wouldn't want his woman to do that. He wants her to accept him as the boss."

Daisy shook his head. "You never did understand me, did you?"

"He doesn't want your hands on him, nor does he want anything else of your skanky ass on him." Maria shoved her away. "Don't even think of coming after him or I will kick your ass."

Daisy laughed, holding on tight to his woman. "We've got nothing to discuss, so I suggest you back off."

They moved away from Laura, and he saw the anger in her eyes. He would bet every last cent of his money that her marriage was dull. It served the bitch right for what she did to him.

"You were amazing," he said, breathing in Maria's scent. She smelled perfect, and his dick grew hard. He wanted inside her badly.

Tonight.

Is she ready?

I hate waiting.

"That's the woman who called you out on who you are?"

"Yes."

"You shouldn't listen to her. She's probably regretting letting her go."

Kissing her neck, Daisy sighed. "It doesn't matter. I was always destined to be with you. Always."

He fucking loved this woman, and even if she didn't allow him to be himself, he'd still love her. Yes, he liked being in charge, and the man who would protect, and look after her, but he liked Maria more than he did that stuff.

"I like you for who you are, Daisy. Don't hold back with me, not once. If you hold back, you're doing yourself a disservice," she said.

"I'm not going to hold back."

They got to their cabin without any more interference from anyone else. With each second that passed, he grew more aroused, wanting to be around her.

Once they entered the cabin, Daisy grabbed her hand, closed the door, and pressed her up against it.

"What you did tonight was fucking hot!"

"You liked me stopping Laura from touching you?" she asked.

He placed his hand between her thighs and started to rub her pussy. She released a moan, arching up against his hand.

"I'm going to fuck you tonight, Maria. I've spent the past week letting you know what I like, and how I like it. Now, I'm going to fuck you, make you scream, and make you beg."

Claiming her lips, Daisy plundered her mouth, taking the kiss he'd been begging for all afternoon.

****

"This is fucking horseshit," Matthew said, storming into Duke's office. It was late Sunday night, and his son had been Prospecting for the past week. He still had school to deal with, but when he finished school, he had to come to the club. Until this was over, Duke was spending all of his spare time at the clubhouse rather than at home. While he was here with his son, Bass, Smash, and Knuckles were taking it turns to take care of his woman.

Holly wasn't happy with the arrangement, but she didn't actually have a choice. This was to help with their son.

"What's horseshit?" Duke asked.

"Dad, he's—"

Duke shook his head. "I'm not your dad right now. I'm Prez, Duke, or Sir."

"Duke, he can't be serious. There's no way I clean the toilets, and then empty the trash bins."

"Excuse me? Who are you accusing you of giving you jobs that are clearly beneath you?" Duke asked.

"Pike, he's ordered me to clean the shit out of the toilets, to go around each room, and empty the trash bins, gather laundry—"

"Pike!" Duke yelled for his VP, and probably his favorite person in that moment.

Pike sauntered into the room, smirking as he took in Matthew. There was none of the usual greeting for his son.

"Landon!" Duke called the other brother as well. Landon was the most recent Prospect turned fully patched member.

Both men were in the office, and the door was still wide enough that anyone close could hear.

"We seem to have a problem. Prospect here seems to think he's too good to clean the toilets, do the laundry, and empty out the trash. Pike, you give him these orders?"

"Yep."

"Prospects don't do this shit," Matthew said.

Landon burst out laughing. "We do, kid. Everyone does this kind of shit. I'm betting Prez and Pike each had to do their time as a Prospect."

"We did. You can't do simple tasks, you've got no chance of making it as a patched in member. In fact, if this was Landon or any other Prospect, I'd take them out back to deal with this shit." Pike stood up, advancing on Matthew.

Duke had to give his son credit. Matthew looked like he was shitting bricks, but he didn't cry, nor did he back down.

"You think Prospecting is about handling a weapon, shooting the shit with the brothers, drinking, and whoring around." Pike grabbed his gun out of the back of his pocket. "This is real shit, Matthew." He pressed the barrel of the gun against his chest. "We're a club, banded together to take care of each other. I know every single one of those fuckers out there would take a bullet for me, and wouldn't even hesitate. Your own father has taken a couple of bullets. This is not some fucking game. This is real life, and you've got a choice, to fight or not to fight, because when it comes down to it, you've got to be ready."

The tension in the room mounted.

Slowly, Pike withdrew his gun. "I will warn you, kid, you want to continue Prospecting with the club, I'm fine with that. It'll make you become a man, but if I give you the job of protecting Mary and my little girl, and anything happens to them, I will kill you. I won't care that I used to babysit you, or shoot hoops with you. I don't even give a fuck that your father is my brother, my Prez, and that I will die for him. You'd be dead without me caring, that's what you've got to be prepared to deal with, you got me?"

Matthew nodded, and Duke dismissed the two men.

Landon stopped near Matthew. "The parties, the women, the drink, the fun, it's all part of it, but to get to that, you've got to be willing to lay down your life. I'm not here all the time, but I've done my fair share for the club. I would die for everyone in this club, and all the old ladies. You've got to be ready to do that before you become a Prospect."

Once they were alone, Duke went back to looking through the charts from the mechanic shop. They were doing well.

"Dad?"

He looked up to see Matthew shaking as he lowered himself into his chair.

"I'm not—"

"I know what you're doing, Dad. You want me to take the options you didn't have, and I get it. I'm going to go to college." Tears filled Matthew's eyes, and he ran a shaky hand down his face. "I wanted to be like you, and like Pike, all the guys. I figured if you could do it, then so could I."

Sitting back in his chair, he stared at his son. For the first time in many months, he truly believed he'd gotten through to him.

"The Trojans will have your back all the time. You're my son, but you've got to earn their respect. They all want what is best for you."

"I just thought I'd get some good sex, and some fun. Holly wants me to go to college, doesn't she?"

"She wants you to have a life that's not bound by the club. You can Prospect in time. You're not ready for this life, Matthew, not yet. You're seventeen. If you don't finish college, then you don't finish college. There will always be a place for you here. You're my son, and I love you."

"Won't they think I'm a wimp?"

Duke shook his head. "We don't allow anyone to Prospect before they're eighteen. I needed you to see what you were getting into. Being a Prospect is no easy feat. When you're ready, there will be no stopping them."

"I'm ready to head home."

"Good. I want to actually sleep next to my wife." He packed away the files, locking them up.

"Do the Prospects only get to clean up the trash?" Matthew asked.

Duke hadn't allowed his son to see what the Prospects went through. For the most part, it was because Matthew was too fucking young. Dyje may be the Prez of the Trojans MC, but there was no way he was going to force the club on his son. Also, there were parts of the club that only a Prospect could see when he had taken a vow to serve and be loyal. Matthew hadn't done that yet.

"Not only do the Prospects not get a chance with the pussy available, they have to watch the club members screw the club women, and they can't join. You'll have to clean the mess up afterward."

Matthew screwed his nose up. "You mean I'd have to clean away their jizz?"

Laughing, Duke nodded. "Yep, and some of them are dirty bastards, and get it everywhere."

They made their way out to his car, and he nodded at several members letting them know their job was done.

Once they were in the car, and he was pulling out of the parking lot, Matthew started talking.

"I do bag my dick up, Dad."

"Good."

"But…"

Duke tensed. "What is it?"

"Before I started Prospecting, I met this girl at school. She's in the same year as me, and one thing led to another."

Duke was getting angry. "What happened?"

"The, er, the condom broke, Dad."

Those words he'd hoped to never have to hear.

"The condom broke."

"Yeah. I'm waiting to hear back from her. Her name is Luna Daniels. What do I do?"

Gripping the steering wheel tightly, Duke counted to ten. What advice should he give his son?

"We're going home, and we're going to talk to Holly about this."

"Luna's not like the other girls, Dad."

No, he didn't imagine she was.

"I've not caught you with her?"

"No. She's not the kind of girl you bang in the car."

"We'll talk to Holly."

"What if I knocked her up?"

"Then we'll handle it."

Duke would handle everything. Damn, he was too young to be a grandfather. Whatever happened, he'd stand by his son, and this girl. He couldn't even picture her, but if she wasn't the kind of girl to screw in the car, he probably hadn't seen her before.

Chapter Nine

Maria moaned as Daisy tore her clothes from her body. There was no way she was going to be able to repair the dress. The straps didn't survive Daisy's strength as he removed them from her body. He tore the bra off, and she was naked before him. Kicking off the shoes, she tugged on his shirt.

"I'm going to fuck you so damn hard tonight, Maria. Once I've taken your cherry, I'm not going to be able to keep my hands from you. You're so fucking beautiful, and you make me want you so badly."

"Yes, please, Daisy, I need your cock inside me. Fuck me, take me, make me yours."

She'd been waiting long enough, and she needed him.

He wrapped his arms around her, stopping her from removing his jeans. Daisy bent forward, caught her up in his arms, and carried her through the cabin.

"What are you doing? Put me down. You're going to hurt yourself." She giggled as he sucked her nipple into his mouth, biting down on the tip. "Ah, that's so good." He moved onto the next nipple, sucking hard before letting her go, and dropping her to the bed.

She released a squeal, and he caught her ankle, keeping her in place.

"I'm in charge here, baby. Don't fight me, and for this first time, you'll do exactly as I say."

Nodding her head, she took a deep breath, lying back on the bed.

"Spread your legs. Show me your creamy cunt."

She loved it when he talked dirty to her.

He opened his belt and started to remove his jeans. His cock sprang forward, and her mouth watered.

Daisy wasn't a small man.

You can take him.

She couldn't wait to fuck him, and to finally be with him properly.

"You want to fuck me, don't you, baby?"

"Yes. I want you."

"From now on, you want to be fucked, you'll come to me, and I will take you. I'll give you everything you need, do you hear me?"

"Yes."

"Good." He wrapped his fingers around the base of his cock, working up to the moist tip. "Do you see this, baby? This is what you do to me. You make me want to fuck you. Being at the club this summer, watching you walk around in your dresses, dancing, you've tortured me with that body of yours."

"Really?" she asked, amazed. "I didn't think you were looking."

"Oh, I was looking, and I can't wait to show you how much I've been looking forward to having some more with you."

"Really?"

"Yes." Daisy smiled. "You're blind, baby. Keeping my hands from you has been difficult. It was hard for me not to come and claim you on the day you graduated. I wanted you that bad, and I knew I could make you happy."

To her, it had always been Daisy, and it would always be him.

He kicked away his jeans and boots. "Touch your pussy."

She touched her pussy with one finger, sliding it across her clit.

"Lift your fingers up, and show me how creamy they are."

Holding her fingers up, she gasped as he caught them and leaned forward. His tongue lapped up her juice.

Suddenly he released her and crooked his finger for her to sit up. Sitting up, she was at the perfect height of his cock. The tip was leaking pre-cum, and she wanted to taste him.

Daisy sank his fingers into her hair and held her in place. "Open those lips."

She did as he ordered, opening her lips, and he placed the tip of his cock against her mouth. When she went to use her tongue, he pulled away.

"No tongue, no teeth. You'll wait for me to tell you what to do."

"Yes, Sir."

He smiled. "Good of you to know your place."

Daisy placed his cock against her lips, and ran the leaking tip across them. "Taste my cum."

She flicked her tongue across, gathering up his pre-cum, and swallowing it.

"Now, lick my cock."

Maria licked his cock, and stared up at him.

He was watching his cock and her lips. His foreskin was peeled back, and she tongued his slit, taking all of his pre-cum. He tugged on her hair, jerking back.

"Your mouth is to fucking die for. Take all of my cock."

She sucked the tip of his cock, and he thrust even more into her mouth. Relaxing her mouth, she took him to the back of the throat, but he didn't stop there. He kept on going until she gagged before pulling out.

"We're going to have to give you more practice on taking my dick, baby."

Maria moaned around the length, loving the way he seemed to swell even more.

Closing her eyes, she gave herself over to him, letting him take his pleasure from her mouth.

Her pussy was on fire, and she reached between her thighs and started to stroke her clit.

"Fuck, baby, don't you know I can see what you're doing? You're touching that pretty little pussy. Sucking my dick is making you all nice and wet, isn't it?"

She hummed her answer.

"That feels so fucking good. Your mouth is perfect." He slowly pumped into her mouth, going in and out.

The grip on her hair tightened, and he pulled out of her mouth. Seconds later, he released her hair and shoved her back to the bed.

"Move up the bed."

Maria didn't question him, and lay against the pillows.

"Open your legs, and hold onto the bars of the bed."

She opened her thighs, and then grabbed two bars, one for each hand.

Looking down at him, she didn't ask any questions, and her heart was pounding. He crawled up the bed, settling between her thighs. Daisy put his hands on either side of her inner thighs, spreading her legs open.

He took the lips of her pussy between his fingers, opening her up.

Maria didn't have time to question him as he took her clit into his mouth and started to suck on her pussy.

She gripped the bars tightly as the pleasure rushed over her, taking her by surprise at the intensity. He'd spent the past week going down on her, and he'd taken a great deal of time finding out what she liked.

This time it was different. He was preparing her for sex.

I'm not going to be a virgin much longer.

She was excited, nervous, but still excited.

Daisy was the man she'd first fallen in love with, and now she was going to belong to him.

Maria had known she'd been in love with him for a long time. The news wasn't shocking to her. She loved him with all of her heart, and that was never going to stop. Her feelings for Daisy had only increased over the summer. He was the one constant, and she would love him for the rest of her life.

He sucked her clit into his mouth, using his teeth to nibble down on the bud.

Using her grip on the bars, she arched up, thrusting her pussy against his face.

"That it, baby, fuck my face, and show me how much you like it." His tongue pressed against her clit, sliding side to side.

The pleasure increased, and she couldn't hold onto her orgasm for much longer. She came apart as he tongued her pussy, but he didn't stop there. Daisy kept on stroking her clit, drawing out another orgasm. Daisy was relentless in his pursuit of giving her orgasm after orgasm.

****

After she had come a second time, and was on the verge of a third orgasm, Daisy used his fingers to prolong her pleasure. He crawled up her body, claiming her lips, and letting her taste her cunt. Daisy hadn't liked licking pussy, but with Maria, it was entirely different. He liked her being his completely. No other man had touched her, and he knew he shouldn't care about that, but he did.

He stopped touching her pussy, grabbed his cock, and placed it at her entrance. Daisy didn't stop to grab a condom as he didn't want anything between them.

Sliding the tip of his cock inside her, he slammed all the way to the hilt. Maria screamed, releasing the bars of the bed, and shoving at his shoulders.

"It's okay, baby, I've got you." He stayed still inside her, giving her a chance to grow accustomed to his cock.

She was unbearably tight.

"You didn't take your time."

"I know." He couldn't have waited even if he wanted to. Maria drove him wild, and her pussy was clutching him deep inside her.

"It hurts."

"I know." This was why he'd tried to avoid actually fucking her. Tears filled her eyes, and he hated the sight of them. Wiping away the drops as they fell cut him deeply.

"I would never hurt you, baby."

"It hurts now."

"I know. I'm sorry."

"Does it hurt for men?"

"No, it doesn't hurt for us."

"We get the short straw again."

Guilt gripped him. "I'd take your pain away if I could."

She sniffled, and he was still upset.

"It'll get better." Leaning down, he kissed her lips. "You're not a virgin anymore, and I heard you complaining to my sister that I hadn't taken the next step."

"You heard that?"

"I came to ask you a question. I left you alone to rant." He rubbed his nose against hers. "How are you feeling now?"

"I don't know. It hurts a little."

He stayed perfectly still, and when this was over, he was going to give himself a reward. The desire to simply fuck her was so strong, but he held off, stopping himself.

"Do you taste your sweet pussy on my lips?"

"Yes."

"I love the taste of you." He kissed her harder, sliding his tongue into her mouth. Time passed, and slowly, Maria started to wriggle beneath him. He didn't know if she noticed it, and he didn't respond right away.

Daisy kissed down her neck, sucking on her pulse. She dug her nails into his shoulders, and she started to thrust against him. He took his time, pulling out of her tight pussy so that only the tip remained inside her, and then he slammed inside.

"Yes!" She screamed the word, and he captured her hands, pressing them beside her head.

"Are you ready for me to fuck you now?" he asked.

"Yes, Daisy, please, fuck me."

Unable to resist her sweet begging, he pulled out of her pussy, taking his time, and relishing the feel of her clenching cunt. Glancing down between them, he saw his cream covered cock, marked with a little of her virgin blood.

She belongs to you now.

You own her.

You must take care of her, and treasure her.

This was what he'd always felt for Maria. She brought out his most protective instincts, and that was never going to disappear.

He was going to love her for the rest of his life, and give her a good life.

"Look at us, baby. Look at my dick fucking your pussy. You belong to me now. I will kill any man who tries to touch you. You'll belong to me all the time."

"Yes, yes, yes."

Releasing her hands, he reared back, grabbing her hips, he started to pound inside her. Maria watched them, and he couldn't pull away.

"I'm going to fill your cunt with my cum, baby." He couldn't wait to see his cum spilling out of her.

Pounding inside her, he made plans for the future, for them to be together.

Maria was always his.

Mine.

Slamming every inch inside her, he dropped her hips, sank his fingers in her hair, and locked his lips against hers. He deepened the kiss, and Maria wrapped her arms around him as he fucked her even harder and deeper. Her tight pussy was a dream come true, and every other woman he'd been with paled in comparison.

This was the woman that was destined to be his. The only woman he wanted to fuck, and to be with.

Wrapping his arms around her, he held her tightly as he filled her pussy with his cum. He came, thrusting to the hilt inside her and groaning. Maria's arms were wrapped around him, holding him tightly.

Mine.

The one word reverberated around his head over and over again. He didn't let go of her even as his orgasm started to fade.

With his arms still wrapped around her, he rolled them over so that he was facing her.

"How are you feeling?" he asked.

"A little sore, but that felt really good." She gave him a huge smile. "I'm not a virgin anymore." She rested her hands on his shoulders. "You didn't wear a condom."

"The moment I took this next step with you there was no turning back." He stroked the pulse beating rapidly in her neck. "No turning back."

"This means I belong to you?"

"You've got that right, baby. You belong to me. You're mine, and I'm not letting you go. Not ever."

"Daisy, I want to tell you something, but I don't think you're ready to hear it."

He smiled. "I love you, Maria."

"What?"

"You don't think I'm going to let you get away with getting in there first, do you?"

"You love me?"

"With all my heart, and I've loved you for a long time. It's never going to change." He pressed a kiss to her lips.

"You stole my words."

"Well, I'd still like to hear them even if they're not original."

"There's nothing original about the words," she said.

"You think so?"

"Everyone says them at least once in their life."

"Yeah, what makes them original, baby, is the way in which they're said. No one is going to say it the same as you. Just like no one is ever going to say it the same way I do. We're original, baby."

She captured his cheek, smiled into his eyes, and he was caught. "Daisy, I love you, and I've loved you my entire life. I saved myself for you."

Claiming her lips, he silenced her words, loving her the only way he could.

Chapter Ten

Three weeks later

Staring around the packed up cabin, Maria felt a little regret to be leaving it. The past four weeks with Daisy had been the best weeks of her life. She stroked her hand over the bare mattress, and wondered when they would be back. The first week, they had learned a great deal about each other. The second week, Daisy had made up for not taking her virginity, and giving her the chance to get accustomed to his touch. After she was no longer sore, Daisy had awakened her entire mind, body, and soul. He'd taken her in ways that she'd only ever dreamed about.

They had gone hiking last week, going down to the river with another picnic. Daisy had made sure she wore a dress that fell to her knees. While they'd been on the blanket, talking, laughing about life, he'd slid his hand up the inside of her skirt. Silence had fallen between them, and Daisy had proceeded to make love to her. First he'd brought her to orgasm with his mouth and fingers. Once she'd screamed his name in climax, he'd taken her hard on the ground, fucking her.

She loved it.

Together they had come in an explosive climax that even remembering it had her wet all over again.

Throughout the cabin, they had fucked, and made love to each other. Daisy had made her straddle his body and ride his cock while he'd been watching a football match on the big screen. He'd been unable to ignore her for long, and had fucked her brains out.

"What's the matter, baby?" Daisy asked, coming up behind her. He wrapped his arms around her waist, pressing a kiss to her neck.

"I don't want to leave."

"Neither do I, but if we don't go, we've got nothing to look forward to. We've got some things to do."

"Like what?"

"Like, I've got to tell your parents that you belong to me. I've also got to let the club know you're my old lady."

Maria closed her eyes. He'd told her the difference between the claiming of an old lady and a club whore. Daisy, during party night, would have to claim her in front of the several members of the club without anyone touching her.

She was so nervous about that, but she'd do it for Daisy. Maria would do anything for him.

"Also, I don't know how Lori is going to respond, and I want to nip any trouble she'd cause in the bud. I've told her there's no chance for us to be together. Lori's a club whore, and Duke has also put her in her place." He kissed her neck. "There's only one woman I want, and you're it." Daisy released her to grab the last bag on the floor. "I'll take this out to the car."

She nodded, following close behind him. They had cleaned and packed everything away so there was no sign of the memories they had made together in the past month.

Leaving the cabin, she turned toward Daisy and was shocked to see Laura there once again.

They hadn't heard from her ever since she had tried to stop them the one night they had dinner with Lucinda and Phil.

Anger filled every part of Maria, and she stormed toward the couple, but they were too busy arguing to see it.

"I made a mistake, Daisy. I want you, and you know you loved fucking me. I can give you everything, not that little girl."

"Fuck off, Laura. You were easy, and I had you because it was easier than going to find another willing pussy. You're not anything special, not by a long shot."

"You think that *girl* can give you what you want?" Laura asked, scathingly.

"That *girl* has just spent the past four weeks of her life giving Daisy everything he needs," Maria said, walking up beside Daisy. She captured his hand, and held him tightly. They were united together as one.

She belonged to Daisy, just like he belonged to her, and that was never going to change.

Laura looked furious. "You really think you're good enough to satisfy him?"

"I've done fine this month."

"You do know he's a control freak, right? He wants you to stay at home, and do all the housework while he's off fucking everything, doing whatever the hell he wants."

Maria laughed. "You never understood what he wants, and don't even think to assume you know what I want."

"As you can see, Laura, I've moved on. I don't want you. I've never wanted you, and I find that you bore me. You bore me more than anyone else I've known. Trying to have sex with me isn't going to cut it here." He gripped the back of Maria's neck, and she sank against him. "This is my woman. This is the woman I love." He tilted her head back, and his mouth was on hers.

She gave herself up to his kiss, and loved him back with a passion that he awoke inside her. There was no one else for her.

"Whatever! It's your loss." Laura stomped away, and Maria couldn't help but chuckle.

"I have to say, Daisy, you know how to pick them."

"Nah, you don't even compare to her, and I picked you." He pressed her against the car, and she wrapped her arms around his neck. "I want to fuck you again."

She moaned. "The cabin is all packed up."

"I'll have to wait until I get you home."

"You mean to the club?"

"No, I mean home. I've got a place. It's an apartment that I've never taken you to. I figured we could go there, drop our stuff off, go to the club, get Beth, and bring her back home."

"I like that. I've missed Beth." This was where she was torn. Beth was her best friend, and she loved her like a sister. Daisy was her man, Beth's brother, and she trusted him to take care of both of them.

"You're wanting to tell me what happened to Beth," he said.

She bit her lip and nodded. What was the point in lying? He knew her, and she didn't want to keep anything from him.

"It's not mine," she said.

He cupped her cheeks. "I won't do anything about it."

"What?"

"You tell me the truth, and I won't do anything. It will be between you and me, no one else."

She held onto his shoulders, glancing at his leather cut.

Tell him.

Benedict deserves what is coming to him.

Beth doesn't want you to tell.

Your friend is dying inside.
You've got to help her.

She was torn apart, scared, petrified, and the truth finally spilled from her lips. "There was a party several months ago. I was too sick to go, but Beth went without me. I'm the one that takes care of our drinks, and, erm, I take care of us. Beth's at times a little party animal. She loved to dance, to party, and to have fun, or at least she used to." They had been completely different, and yet no one could tear them apart. She loved Beth with all of her heart, and she wouldn't do anything to hurt her friend. "I didn't hear from Beth to say she got home, and the following morning, when I hadn't heard from her, I got out of bed. I was so sick, but I forced myself to drive to Benedict's place." She'd had to pull over multiple times to lean out of the car in case she was sick. "I found Beth naked in one of the spare guest rooms. She was freaking out, and she was terrified. Benedict was there, taunting her that she should learn to hold her liquor. Beth had only had one drink, and because she'd taken it from someone, she broke the cardinal rule we had. No drinks from anyone. Someone spiked her drink, and she was date raped. Beth was aware the whole time, but she just couldn't do anything while it happened."

Saying the words allowed filled her with dread, and when she looked into Daisy's eyes, she knew he was struggling to hold it together.

"Someone date raped my sister, and that fucker is still breathing?" he asked.

"Daisy?"

"No, fucking no. Get in the fucking car."

He stormed around to his side of the car, and climbed inside.

She had made a huge mistake. "You promised you wouldn't do anything."

"I thought some asshole broke her heart. I'm not having some prick think he can take what he wants, and get away with it."

He pulled the cell phone up, and Maria gritted her teeth as he started to call his parents. She saw the number on the cell phone.

"What's the matter—"

"She was fucking raped!"

"Daisy," his father said.

"No, fuck you, and fuck this little shit. His days are numbered, Dad. You should have told me."

"There wasn't enough evidence. Beth had already washed a great deal of it away, and there were more witnesses to say she went willingly—"

"You believe that crock of shit?"

"It doesn't matter what I believe. It's what the courts, lawyers, and the law believe. I wasn't willing to drag Beth through the mud as it wasn't guaranteed we'd win."

"This is fucking horseshit."

Daisy hung up the phone, and the next, she saw the club number.

Covering her face with her hands, Maria knew she had made a huge mistake, and now she may have lost the man she loved along with her best friend. Daisy wouldn't let Benedict live after what he knew, and Beth was never going to trust her again.

****

Daisy pulled into the clubhouse parking lot, and like he'd planned, his brothers were ready to ride with him. None of them believed in forcing a woman, and today they were going to avenge his little sister. Beth had always been the fun time girl, but she didn't deserve to have her will taken from her.

"Don't do this," Maria said.

127

He had truly believed the big secret had been some big crush that went wrong. Instead, he had to learn that his sister had been hurt in one of the worst ways possible, and that shit wouldn't stand with him.

Beth stood by the door, and she gave him a wave, even though she looked confused.

Climbing out of the car, he moved toward her, and she backed away.

"Some fucker raped you?"

"Who told you?" Her gaze moved toward Maria.

"I'm really sorry."

Beth sighed. "It's nothing."

"Don't fucking say shit like that. This fucker, his days are numbered, and you should have come to me."

He moved away from his sister, and paused right in front of Maria. Her tears twisted his gut, and he hated seeing them. Cupping her cheek, he slammed his lips down on hers, and claimed her lips. His body wanted inside her, and he didn't hate her for keeping Beth's secret. Daisy was more pissed at his sister for keeping it a secret. This was not Maria's fault, and it never would be. This was on Beth, not on Maria.

"I love you. This doesn't change anything."

"You promised me you wouldn't do anything."

"This can't be allowed to stand." He kissed her again, and walked toward his bike.

"Good to have you back, brother," Knuckles said.

Several of his brothers nodded at him, and he climbed on his bike. It was time to travel back to his hometown. It would only take a few hours, but the tension running through his veins wouldn't let up. He needed to hurt this bastard, and his father had promised to show him who Benedict was.

****

"I'm so sorry," Maria said, walking toward her friend.

"It's okay."

"No, it's not okay. I shouldn't have said anything. I'm the worst friend in the world." Maria wiped away her tears, regretting what she had done.

"It was only a matter of time before something like this happened."

"I'm really sorry."

Beth gave her a sad smile. "I should have told him, Maria."

It didn't matter what Beth said. Maria would forever have this guilt. Moving toward the trunk of the car, Maria grabbed her cases out.

"What are you doing?"

"I can't stay here. I trusted Daisy, and I broke your trust in me."

"You didn't break my trust, Maria."

Maria shook her head. "I can't stay here." She didn't want to deal with Daisy after he did whatever he had to do.

"Where are you going to go?" Beth asked.

"I don't know. I'd find somewhere." Her case was already packed, and when she walked in she saw Holly and Mary taking care of their kids.

Maria paused, staring at the two friends.

"You don't have to leave," Holly said

"Daisy will come hunting for you," Mary said.

"He won't, and now he's going to go and hurt someone. I shouldn't have said anything. It was a pleasure meeting both of you, and I will miss the two of you." She gave each woman a hug, and moved back toward her old room. Grabbing the last of her stuff, she walked into Beth's room, to grab her fully charged cell phone.

There were only two people she could call, and even though she had never felt like she belonged with them, there was nowhere else for her to go.

She listened to the phone ring, and wondered if they would answer.

"Hello," her father said, answering the call.

"Hey, Daddy," she said, sobbing.

"Maria? Honey, what's wrong?"

****

Several hours later, Daisy and his brothers were at a bar in town, known as one of Benedict's haunts. After visiting with his father, and getting some information about this fucker, it seemed that Benedict was known for sticking roofies to girls, and there's always no evidence other than the girl being a party animal.

Knuckles stepped beside him. "We going to kill?"

"Nah, I think this fucker is too damn special to kill. We're going to let him live, only he's going to live with a very different way of life."

Duke, Pike, Raoul, and Crazy had come with him and Knuckles to the bar. The rest of his brothers were paying a visit to Benedict's parents, and were going to give them a warning.

Diaz, Raoul's friend, and computer expert, had already given him the details to keep the parents quiet. It would seem they were not exactly legal in some of their business ventures. Diaz had found out the truth, and now, all he needed to do was have a nice long word with Benedict.

There was a woman at the bar, who was cleaning out a glass. He saw on her badge that her name was Cindy.

"Can I help you men?" she asked.

"Yeah, bottles of beer all around, and you can tell us what you know about big time Benedict," Daisy said, taking a seat.

Cindy tensed up. "Benedict."

"We heard he guarantees he doesn't take no for an answer. You heard the rumor?" Knuckles asked.

She looked uncomfortable and took a deep breath. "I've heard rumors, but I've never seen him actually do it. Erm, there's been some women here who would come for some fun, and then never come back." Cindy looked at him. "You're Daisy, Beth's brother?"

"Yes, you remember me?"

"Vaguely. Benedict has always been a spoilt bastard, and telling everyone he can have whoever the hell he wanted. Beth, she always showed him her disdain. She couldn't stand him, and yet he bragged about bagging her."

Knuckles slammed his hand down on the bar, making Cindy cry out.

"You believe that shit?"

"No, I didn't believe it. I don't want to serve the creep, but I need this job more." Cindy bit her lip. "He's not come in tonight yet. He'll be here around nine, maybe a little later."

"He waits until a couple of women are already smashed with drink," Duke said. "This bastard sounds like a real prince."

"He's not, and he's dangerous. His family owns some kind of company that means no one goes after him. He's protected, and he's the Mayor's son." Cindy handed them bottles of beer.

"We're not here to cause trouble, Cindy."

"Will you tell your sister, I believed her? She left town, and I think she did because no one behaved like they believed her."

"Don't worry, Cindy. By the end of tomorrow, everyone is going to believe my sister." He gave her a wink, and spun to face the door.

"Man, I can't wait to see the son of a bitch," Pike said.

Daisy counted to ten as he stared at the door. It would only be a matter of time before this fucker came through the door, and when he did, Daisy couldn't wait to make his night awful.

Sipping his beer, he smiled as, right on time, Benedict came through the door with a couple of his friends.

It was going to be a fun night.

Chapter Eleven

Her parents were waiting for her when she got back home. Daisy was out looking for Benedict, and she doubted he would come looking for her. What if he was caught murdering Benedict? When her mother and father pulled her against them, Maria sobbed.

"I love him," she said.

They entered her childhood home, and Maria stared around, wondering why she had come to them. Her mother and father had never enjoyed her company.

"I'm going to go make some hot chocolate," her mother said.

Sitting on the sofa in the sitting room, she was shocked to see her graduation photo. Beth's father had taken it, and Maria stood between her parents. At the time she hadn't thought she made them proud, but seeing the look in their eyes they had been.

"So, tell me what is going on," her father said.

Maria told him everything, about what happened to Beth. She explained going to the club, and then being with Daisy, all the way up to what happened this morning. Her father listened, and when her mother came in, she listened as well.

She watched as her mother perched on the arm of the chair, and her father placed his hand on her hip. The love between the two was strong.

"Daisy's gone to handle Benedict?" her mother asked.

"Yes. The whole club has."

"About fucking time." Her father snapped out the words.

"What?"

"I never liked that boy, and he's always been an entitled prick. Do you know how much I fucking hated that boy? Every time you left the house, I lived in fear of you being near him, or him looking at you."

Maria was shocked. She didn't think her parents cared all that much. "You were worried?"

"Of course we were worried," her mother said.

She looked at her parents, mouth open, shocked. "That's not right," she said.

They shared a look, and Maria wondered what she was missing.

"We've failed you, honey." Her father looked toward his wife, and sighed. "For most of your life, we have not been the best parents that we could be, and that is our fault. You were always trying to be the best you could be."

"We had you at a young age, and neither of us knew what to do," her mother said. "This summer that you've been gone, your father and I, we have taken time to think, and we were ashamed, honey."

"We should have been here more, protected you more." Her father spoke up.

"Instead, we pushed you aside, making you feel like you weren't loved, when that is not the truth," her mother said.

"We love you, and we wanted to protect you. Daisy helped to open our eyes," her father said.

"Daisy?"

"Yes. He called us, and pretty much gave us a list of where we were failing you." Her father stood up, walking toward her. He lowered down to his knees, and cupped her cheek. "You're a beautiful, stunning daughter, and I am proud that I helped raise you. I'm hoping that you can forgive me for not showing you how much I love you sooner."

Tears fell from her eyes, and she wrapped her arms around him tightly. "I love you, Daddy."

"I hope you can forgive us." Her mother moved up beside her, stroking her cheek. "Now, let's get you some soup, or something else, and then you're going to bed for rest. I imagine Daisy will be coming back to take you with him. That boy could never stay away long." Her mother once again walked away, and Maria frowned.

"What did she mean about Daisy not being able to stay away?"

Her father chuckled. "You never saw the way Daisy looked at you. He was always taking care of you. I remember when you were trying to ride your bike."

"Daisy told me. You were getting angry with me, and I was disappointing you."

"You didn't disappoint me. I didn't know what I was doing wrong. You weren't trusting me. I went in to talk to your mother to see what I could do to help you, and then I watched as Daisy walked up behind you. He spoke, and the next moment, you were riding. The first time I've ever been jealous of another boy. He was able to help my daughter, and I couldn't. It was not very welcoming."

Wiping away her tears, Maria threw her arms around her father. "I love you."

"I love you, too, honey. If I was ever going to trust a man with you, it would be Daisy. He loves you."

"I love him. I love him so much."

"Then let him come back to you. He's got to do this for his sister. I don't know much about MCs other than what I see on the television, but he needs to do this, and I would be proud to call him my son-in-law."

Holding onto her father, Maria felt whole once again. Now, all she needed was for Daisy to forgive her.

****

Daisy watched as Benedict took a seat next to a table full of women. He saw the reaction from most of the women, and that was mainly disgust. They didn't like him being close to them, and that he could understand.

"That's the fucker who hurt Beth?" Knuckles asked.

"The one and only."

"I've had enough of this. I've got a son who could have knocked up a girl, and I need to get back to Vale Valley. I'm not going to prolong this," Duke said.

"Huh?" Daisy asked. "Matthew's gotten a girl pregnant?"

"I don't know. Holly and I are waiting for the girl in question to let us know."

"Have you met her?" Pike asked.

"I've not. Holly has, and of course Matthew has. They're keeping it quiet in case nothing is wrong." Duke looked frazzled. "I'm too damn young to be a grandfather."

Daisy didn't want to prolong this either. Placing his beer back on the counter, he walked up to the table, and took a seat. His brothers gathered around him, and the girls on the next table took their cue to leave.

"Hello, Benedict," Daisy said, staring at the fucker who really believed he'd gotten away with raping his sister.

"I don't know who you are." Benedict looked from him to his brothers behind him. "Are you an investor?" The bastard snorted, and Daisy burst out laughing. His brothers started laughing as well, giving him the lead on what to do with this fucker.

"I'm Beth's big brother."

Silence met his statement.

"Not laughing now!" Daisy raised his brow, and he wasn't surprised when the two friends started to leave.

Glancing back at Cindy, he waited for her to either nod or shake her head. She shook her head, and he allowed the men to go.

"Where the fuck are you two going?" Benedict asked.

"This is your problem, not ours."

"Well, well, well, your friends soon scatter. I wonder why that is."

"Look, man, I don't know what Beth—"

Daisy didn't even allow him to finish. Grabbing the bastard's head, he slammed his face down on the table. "Don't even fucking go there. Let's go and see what we can do about this." Holding the bastard's collar he started to pull him out of the bar. His brothers would have his back. He shoved him to the dirt in front of him, outside of the bar.

"You raped my fucking sister. Stuck a roofie in her glass, and then took what didn't belong to you." He dropped him to the floor and slammed his fist against the bastard's face.

"She wanted it."

Benedict tried to land a blow, but this bastard had messed with the wrong crowd.

Over and over, Daisy landed blow after blow, and when he couldn't stand the thought of this man touching any woman, he stomped on his genitals.

"You're not going to get away with this," Benedict said, gasping, and squeaking out.

Glancing toward his club brothers, they all nodded.

"Your parents have washed their hands of you. They want nothing more to do with you. Your days are over, you fucking bastard."

The sound of a cop car in the distance had Daisy pausing. Benedict was in a bad shape. "You're going to admit to the rape of Beth, and you're also going to admit to all the women you've taken."

"Why would I do that?"

"If you don't, I will make sure your life a living hell. I can strap you to the back of my bike, and make you drive all the way back to Vale Valley with me. Your parents want nothing to do with you, and I will make sure that I spend every day finding a man who's willing to fuck your ass every single hour, of every single day. You've got great parents there, Benedict. The moment their fortune and their own reputation were put on the line, they dropped you fast than a hot fucking saucepan. It seems your parents are not exactly making money the legal way, are they? Drugs? They want their money more than they wanted you. If I can't find anyone to use you in jail, I'll use my fucking bat to fuck you."

Benedict whimpered. "Yes, I'll do it. I'll do it."

Stepping back, Knuckles came forward, grabbing Benedict's head. "Time for you to shine."

****

Daisy entered the clubhouse the following morning. His knuckles were bloodied, and he was so fucking tired. Duke, Pike, Raoul, and Crazy had gone home to their women, and the brothers without one had come back to the clubhouse.

Beth left the kitchen, and she looked at him, and then past his shoulder toward Knuckles.

"Dad call you?"

"Yes. So did the sheriff who took Benedict's confession. You beat him to confession?"

"It's the least I could do. You don't keep anything from me, no matter what." He walked toward her, wrapping his arms around her. Beth let go, sobbing into his arms.

"It was my fault."

"No, it wasn't your fault."

"I shouldn't have wanted to party."

He captured her face and wiped away her tears. "You had every single right to party, and to have fun. No one had the right to take that away from you." He held onto his sister, knowing he would die protecting her. Thinking of the other woman he'd die for, he started looking around the clubhouse. "Where's Maria?"

"You've not checked your cell phone, have you?" Beth asked.

"No, why would I?"

"Maria left."

"What?" His heart started to race.

"She felt so guilty, and she left."

"Where the fuck did she go?"

"She went home."

"Back home?" Where he'd just ridden back from?

"Yes. She texted me that she made it home."

Cursing, he spun on his heel, and headed toward the door.

"Where are you going?" Knuckles asked.

"I'm going to go and get my stubborn woman." He looked toward his sister. "She's my old lady, and she will be my wife. Can you handle that?"

Beth smiled. "Of course I can handle that."

Looking toward Knuckles, he gave him a nod. "Take care of her, and don't touch her."

Daisy wasn't stupid. He had no doubt that Knuckles had a thing for his sister, and he would handle it the moment he crossed the line.

For now, he had to go and get his woman back.

****

Beth sat in her bedroom as she stared down at her cell phone. She had yet to enroll in a college nearby, and now the entire club knew what happened to her. Between her and Maria, she had always been the partier. She loved dancing and having fun. Once Benedict burst her bubble, she'd been withdrawn, afraid to let go. After all, look what happened the last time she let go.

Someone knocked on her door, and she knew it wouldn't be Daisy and Maria. He'd left twenty minutes ago.

"Come in," she said.

Knuckles opened the door, and she expected to see disgust or pity in his eyes. When she stared at him, she saw nothing. He simply stared at her. "How are you?" he asked.

"I'm okay. Hoping Maria and Daisy can work things out."

"They will. They're meant to be together." He closed the door and moved toward her.

"What are you thinking?" she asked.

"I'm wondering why you're here, and not out there with the rest of the guys."

She closed her cell phone and ran her fingers through her hair. "You know, and they know. You all know what happened, and I just, I just can't think about that right now."

Knuckles sighed. "You're no different to me."

"I'm not?" She turned toward him, and sighed. "You're not seeing someone damaged or broken right now?"

"No. I'm seeing a woman who is scared to be herself, but I also see a woman who is scared of what others think around her." Knuckles took hold of her chin, and turned her head so that she had no choice but to face him. "You've got nothing to fear with me or with the brothers. What happened, happened. You don't need to hide who you are."

"I'm not hiding."

"Yeah, you are." He stroked his thumb across her lip. "You and I, we're going to happen. It won't be today, it may not even be this year, but we're going to go down that road. You can feel it, just like I can." He closed the distance between them, pressing his lips against hers.

Beth froze at the contact, even though she liked his touch.

Knuckles pulled away. "In time, you're going to see there's nothing to be afraid of."

"What about my brother?"

"I've always lived dangerously. Your brother is going to get pissed with me, but that I can handle."

****

Holly stood beside Matthew as they waited for Luna to get out of the bathroom. Duke was at the clubhouse, and he was waiting for her call. She couldn't believe she was actually waiting to find out if her son— and she saw Matthew as her son—was going to be a father.

"You must be really disappointed with me," he said.

Glancing over at him, she saw he looked terrified. A few weeks ago, he was laughing about this kind of shit, screwing girls, and not going to college. He had talked about joining the Trojans MC, and she hadn't cared about it at all. She just wanted him to have a choice, and Duke felt the same way. Matthew had so much potential, and she didn't want him to live with regrets.

"I'm not disappointed. I just hope you learn from what you're going through. You're too young to be doing this kind of shit." Holly folded her arms beneath her breasts. Luna was not the girl she had expected Matthew to hook up with. She'd seen the porn magazines, the search history on the internet, and even the girls he'd dated. They had all been slender, blonde, beautiful, and everything that epitomized Matthew.

Luna was a beautiful girl. She had brown hair that was pulled back into a ponytail. She wore glasses, and she was fuller than a lot of the girls. The way Matthew looked at her, there was something there.

"If she's not pregnant, she's never going to talk to me," Matthew said.

"You don't know that."

"She hasn't spoken to me since that night, Holly. She doesn't want anything to do with me, and I can't blame her."

Before she had a chance to say anything, the door opened, and Luna held up the pregnancy test. Her hand was shaking, and she took a deep breath. "It's negative. Can I go home now?"

Luna brushed past them, and Matthew looked so disheartened. "Luna, wait."

Holly stayed back knowing this was between the young couple. "Nothing happened. I'm not pregnant, and you don't need to worry about being tied to me. I don't want to be tied to you either, Matthew. I've got a life I want to live. Please don't talk to me anymore."

With that, Luna turned on her heel, and left.

Chapter Twelve

Maria lay in her bed, staring at the photograph of her and Beth. Behind the camera was Daisy, and even though she couldn't see him, Maria remembered he was there. In the photo they were about fifteen, and had just gotten back from the lake.

Tears spilled from her eyes over what she had lost. She had loved Daisy forever, and now she had lost him.

Maybe you overreacted.

You ran because you were afraid of Daisy falling out of love with you.

She didn't know what to make of what happened. Her parents had kept her company until she had gone to bed. It had been strange being with them as they were attentive to her. Part of her missed the way they used to ignore her, which only made her feel even guiltier. All of her life she'd wanted to be noticed by them, and now she wanted to forgotten by them.

Putting the photo back on the drawer beside her bed, she settled back down, wiping away her tears. Sniffling, she rolled over so that she was facing the window. Closing her eyes, she started to count sheep when all of a sudden there was a loud banging coming from the front door.

"Maria!"

Her name was yelled, and she lifted up in bed, wondering if she had heard it.

"Maria! Open the door."

Climbing out of bed, she opened her door, and saw both of her parents leaving their room. They were in robes, and she was in her pajama shorts and a tank top.

"Who is it?" her mother asked.

She knew who it was. "It's Daisy."

"Do you want me to handle this, honey?" her father asked.

"Maria, baby, open the door. I'm not going anywhere."

Releasing a sigh, she shook her head. "I can handle this."

"Are you sure?"

"I'm sure." She walked down the stairs, and at the door, she hesitated.

You can do this.

You love him.

You want to be with him.

Opening the door, she stared at him. His hand was raised to knock again.

"What are you doing here?" she asked.

"You're not at the clubhouse, and you're mine, Maria."

"You were angry with me."

"No. I wasn't angry with you. I was angry for being a total ass. Out of everything that happened to Beth, I didn't for one second believe it was that." He pushed the door open, and wrapped his arm around her waist. "What are you doing back here?"

"She's my daughter, Daisy. She can come back home whenever she wants." Her father was standing at the stairs with her mother behind him.

"Could have fooled me," Daisy said. "I remember a time you couldn't stand to be around her."

Maria saw the hurt look on her parents' faces, and she felt guilty.

"We made a mistake, and we will be making up for that for the rest of our lives," her mother said.

"I'm going to be marrying your daughter," Daisy said. "I'm going to marry her, provide for her, and love her for the rest of our lives. I expect your full support."

"You love her?" her father asked.

"Yes, I love her."

"Then I've got no complaints. I always knew you were going to be more than just her best friend's brother." Her father turned looked toward her. "Are you happy?"

"Yes."

"Then we will leave you to make up." Her father urged her mother upstairs, leaving them alone.

Daisy still had his arm wrapped around her waist and was pulling her close.

"You left the clubhouse."

"I thought you hated me for keeping that secret, and not telling you. It was Beth's secret, but it was so huge. I mean, she was raped, and I didn't tell you. I didn't tell anyone."

He slammed his lips down on hers, and slid his tongue into her mouth. She melted against him, loving the raw possession of his mouth on hers. He grabbed her ass, tugging her in close.

"We can't do this here," she said. "It's my parents' house."

"Then get your shit, and get on my bike."

Running from him, she rushed toward her bedroom, and quickly threw on a pair of jeans. Packing a bag of clothes, she knocked on her parents' door letting them know she wouldn't be around.

"Thank you. I'm heading back to Vale Valley with Daisy. I love you."

"Are you sure?" his father asked.

"Yes. I love him."

"I look forward to getting the invitation."

She rushed downstairs to find Daisy on his bike waiting. Climbing on behind him, she wrapped her arms around his waist, and rested her cheek against his back. "Take me home."

"When you're with me, we're always home."

Closing her eyes, she held onto Daisy as he rode back toward the clubhouse, and to their future.

****

Daisy was tired, exhausted, but he had his woman, and he was determined to fuck her. It was early morning, and he didn't stop to look at any of his club brothers. He nodded at them, and kept on walking with Maria in front of him. With his hands on her shoulders, he moved her toward his bedroom. There was time for everything else later.

"You're being rude," she said.

"No, your pussy is going to be wrapped around me." The moment the door to his room was closed, he removed his leather cut. "Get your ass naked."

Within seconds he was naked, and he helped her get rid of the clothes that were in his way. Pressing her to the bed, he took possession of her lips, and ran his hands up and down her body.

"I fucking love you," he said.

"I love you, too, and yes, I'm going to marry you."

"I wasn't asking." He was going to marry Maria even if he had to force her. "You're mine, you'll always be mine, and that's never going to change."

Sliding his fingers between her thighs, he slammed two fingers inside her cunt, feeling her tighten around him.

"See, this pussy is mine, and it was made for me. My pussy, made for me," he said. Lifting his fingers to his mouth, he tasted her cream, and moaned around them. "So tasty."

He couldn't wait, and kissing down her body, he paused when he was above her pussy. Cupping her ass, he took her clit into his mouth, and sucked the swollen nub into his mouth. Releasing her ass with one of his hands, he pressed a finger into her cunt. She squeezed him tightly, and he ran them down between the cheeks of her ass. He pressed his fingers against her ass, and pressed into the tight ring of muscles.

"Daisy?"

"Trust me, baby. I'm going to fuck this ass, and you're going to love it." He pressed past the right ring of muscles, and filled her ass with one of his fingers.

"Fuck, that feels so good," she said.

Nibbling down on her clit, he used his teeth to draw her pleasure out even more. "I'm going to claim you in front of the club by the end of the week, Maria. I'm not going to wait any longer. You're all mine, and I want every single brother to know that you belong to me."

"I love you, Daisy. I'll do whatever you want me to do. I want to be yours."

Sliding his fingers in and out of her ass, he plundered her pussy with his tongue, moaning as the taste of her exploded.

She was so wet and juicy.

"Yes, yes, yes," she said, panting his name.

He fucked his tongue inside her, flicking up to stroke over her clit.

"So tasty, and so good."

When he didn't know if he was going to last much longer, he stroked her even harder. Within seconds she cried out his name, and he didn't stop bringing her to orgasm.

Once she came down from her orgasm, he released his fingers from her ass, slamming his dick deep inside her cunt.

She cried out, screaming his name.

"That's it. Shout my name. It's me that is fucking you, no one else. No one else is going to know how damn tight you are, and how fucking perfect you are. You belong to me, no one else."

"Yes, please, Daisy, fuck me."

"Tell me you want me," he said.

"I want you."

"You're going to be my wife?"

"Yes."

Pounding inside her dripping cunt, he claimed her lips. He was never going to let her go. Daisy was going to love her forever until the day they died.

****

"So, they're not pregnant?" Duke asked, climbing into bed.

"No. They're not pregnant, and next week, he'll start going to college talks. I've gotten several of them to write to Matthew," Holly said, rolling over.

"I never want to have a girl."

She chuckled. "You've not got much choice. We're got what we've been given." Taking hold of his hand, she placed it over her stomach. "And we've got another baby on the way." With everything that had been happening with Matthew, she hadn't known how to break the news to her man. Duke was distracted by club business and by their son.

"We're pregnant again?"

"Yes. I don't know what we've got. It could be a girl."

"Fuck, I could have a girl. We're going to have another baby? Is everything okay?"

"Everything is fine. I'm already taking my folic acid, and I've got an appointment next week."

Duke claimed her lips before sliding down the bed. "Be a boy, please be a boy."

Holly laughed. "Matthew's upset."

"What?"

"Luna doesn't want anything to do with him, and has asked him to stay away from her. She's upset." Holly felt sorry for Matthew, but she didn't know what he expected. You don't just sleep with a girl, and move onto the next, expecting one of them wait for you.

"He's going to be taking some hard knocks for the rest of his life."

"I think he loved Luna, maybe still does."

"He's too young to find love."

"Do you really believe that?" Holly asked.

"I don't know. I know I love you, and I'd die for you."

"You're just trying to get into my panties."

"Babe, I've been getting into your panties for the past three years, and I'm looking forward to getting into them for the all the years of our life."

Holly snorted. "You're no charmer, but you're my mine."

Cupping his cheek, she kissed him back. She really did love this man with her whole heart and soul.

She would die for him as well.

Chapter Thirteen

Maria watched as Daisy played pool with Knuckles. She sat with Beth, and it was a Friday night, party night. This was the night he had promised her that she was going to be taken as his old lady in the eyes of the club. Her pussy was soaking wet, and she couldn't help but keep looking around the whole room at all of the men waiting in the room. Were they going to want to see?

"I love your ring," Beth said, pointing at her ring.

Glancing down, Maria couldn't help but smile. Daisy had given her the ring the next day after he'd brought her back to the club. He had also told her what happened to Benedict, and what they had gotten from him.

"I love him."

"I'm really pleased."

"Benedict admitted to what he did," Maria said. Her parents had called her to let her know what was happening in the town.

"Yeah, and it took him getting a beating from my brother for him to admit to it. Benedict's parents have also refused to help him out. Daisy told me it was because the club had some bad information about them, and they were going to use it unless they backed off." Beth rubbed her head. "He shouldn't have done it."

"From what Daisy told me, you're not the only woman he preyed on," she said.

Tears filled her eyes as she turned to her friend. Beth was pale and sad. "I'm going to call it a night. I'm tired."

"Beth?" Maria said.

"I'm fine, and I'm happy for you. I enrolled in the college just outside of Vale Valley. I start in two weeks."

They had moved out of the club, but Beth hadn't wanted to leave. Daisy didn't like leaving her at the Trojans MC clubhouse, but they couldn't force her to live with them. Knuckles kept a constant eye on her, and so far he hadn't crossed that line. She knew Daisy was keeping an eye on Beth, but there was only so much he could do as a brother.

She gave Beth a hug, and she felt bad for not being able to do more for her friend. Sitting on her seat, she watched as Beth gave her brother a hug, and then there was a look shared between Beth and Knuckles, making her wonder what her friend was thinking.

Knuckles was the first man she had seen Beth show any interest in. He was also a dangerous man. Maria had listened to the club whores talk, and what they had to say left her feeling uneasy.

Beth left, and the two men went back to playing their game. During the next hour, Maria became aware of several brothers leaving so that there were only a few brothers left. She bit her lip seeing Holly, Mary, Duke, and Pike sitting in the corner.

Were they going to watch?

She took a sip of the soda that she'd had for the past hour, and it had gone warm. Was it getting hotter, or was it just her?

Crap. Her life was getting complicated, and she hated that.

"I won, man," Daisy said, dropping the pool stick on the table.

This was it? Was this it?

Daisy moved toward her, stashing some cash in the back pocket of his jeans. He placed his hand on her thigh, sliding underneath her skirt.

Heat filled her body as he grazed her pussy.

"Hey, baby, come and dance with me."

He moved his hand away from between her thighs, and tugged her off the stool.

"What about, erm, the you know?"

Daisy chuckled. "Let it happen. Focus on me, no one else."

He moved her toward the center of the room, and started to dance with her. She closed her eyes, enjoying the feel of being surrounded by him. The club faded away so that all that was left were the two of them.

"I imagined this," she said.

"What?"

"Being in your arms, loving you, being part of this, and your world."

"You were always supposed to be mine, baby." She tilted her head back, and he took possession of her mouth. "I love you."

"I love you, too." She whispered the words against his lips, and one of his hands started to slide down to cup her ass. She gasped as he rubbed his cock against her stomach. Closing her eyes, she gave herself over to the pleasure.

Music filled the room, and she focused on Daisy's arms as he moved her toward one of the sofas near the wall. It was thick, and he spun her around until she had to kneel on the sofa. In front of her was a mirror that showed her the room behind her. She saw the club members as they watched them.

"They're not going to touch you, baby. They know you belong to me, and that I don't share. You're mine, and I'll never give you up." He opened her shirt, and cupped one of her breasts. "You're a fucking dream come true."

His other hand slid between her thighs, teasing her slit.

"So wet and creamy. You're fucking beautiful, baby." He plunged two fingers inside her pussy, and she fucked herself onto him, taking him as deep as she could go.

Daisy was driving her crazy with need, and there was nothing she could do to stop it, nor did she want to. He was the love of her life, the master of her heart.

He released her long enough to unbutton his jeans, and press the naked tip of his cock against her cunt. The head of him pushed in an inch, and then one of his hands was on her hip while the other gripped her tit.

Slamming every single inch of his dick inside her, Daisy took her in the eyes of the club.

"Open your eyes, baby. They're watching as I take you."

She opened her eyes and saw the men staring at them. Daisy didn't stop as he fucked her deeply, and she loved it. The men's eyes were assessing, but none of them looked lustfully at them. There was a respect, a knowledge, and an understanding. She belonged to Daisy. She would always belong to him.

"Mine, Maria. You're fucking mine."

He pounded inside her, startling her with the ferocity of his claiming.

"Touch your pussy. Come all over my cock, and then I'll fill you with my spunk."

She reached between them, touching her pussy, and biting her lip.

"Don't you stop those screams. I want to hear you come, baby. Scream for me, and let me hear how well I'm fucking you, and I love it." He slammed inside her, over and over again, never letting up.

Touching her clit, she stroked herself, bringing her closer and closer to orgasm. She screamed his name as she erupted.

Daisy sank his fingers into her hair, tugged on the length, and started biting her neck with kisses.

He fucked her hard and raw, and she loved every second of it. When he came, he came hard and deep, making her moan for more.

She didn't know what she expected after it was over, but Daisy pulled out of her pussy, covered her body, and tidied himself before picking her up in his arms. He carried her out of the main room, and away from the men.

"Did I do something wrong?" she asked.

"No. The club knows you're my old lady, and now I get to have you to myself for the rest of the night."

He kicked his door closed, and laid her on the bed. She watched as he stripped out of his clothes, and then got her naked.

The moment he slid inside her once again, Maria was ready for him.

"I'm going to love you for the rest of my life," he said.

She cupped his cheek, knowing she was the luckiest woman in the world.

****

One week later

Beth walked out of the clubhouse with her bag on her shoulder. College had already started, and she didn't trust herself to live on campus. She liked having a permanent place within the clubhouse. It was probably wrong seeing as she wasn't screwing any of the men, but she helped to clean the clubhouse, and also, she paid Duke rent. There was no way she was ready to have a relationship with anyone.

Her best friend was planning her wedding, and Beth wanted to be part of it all. Zipping up her jacket, she folded her arms across her chest, and started toward the bus stop.

The sound of the bike coming up behind her had her freezing to the spot.

"What are you doing?" Knuckles asked, stopping beside her.

He hadn't pushed, not once had he pushed her for anything other than company. They played video games into early in the morning. He was always in the background, providing her a safety net that was also terrifying her.

"I'm walking to the bus stop."

"You never take the bus to college. Jump on."

"I really need to learn to take the bus. I can't expect you to, erm, be around for me every moment of every day."

Knuckles removed his glasses and stared at her. "Do you want me to lose my shit with you right now?"

"Look, when you get bored with me, I'm going to have to use the bus anyway. I'd prefer to do it now."

He climbed off his bike and stalked toward her. "What the fuck are you saying?"

"I don't know what your problem is."

"My problem is you thinking I would simply push you aside when I got bored. In case you don't know, I never get bored, and I'm not going to start getting bored. Now, get on the back of my fucking bike before I put you over my knee and spank your ass. When I picked you up this afternoon I was going to take you for some apple pie, but this time, you've not been good enough."

She couldn't help the little lift of pleasure from his admission, and then it crashed. Knuckles knew the best places to get the best food. She didn't want to miss that. "I'm sorry."

"I told you once, we're happening, whether you like it or not. We're going to happen, Beth. You're going to be my woman, and I'm going to take care of you."

"I'm not ready. We're friends."

"When you're ready, I'll be there. I'm in here right now." He pointed at her head. "Soon, I'm going to be in here, and then I'm going to be inside you, fucking you, making you mine." He startled her as he leaned in kissing her lips. "Now, get back on the fucking bike."

Her heart raced with pleasure, with nerves, with everything.

Knuckles was invading her mind, and it scared her. He inspired feelings she wasn't ready to face, but what scared her more was the feeling he was never going to go away. He'd gotten inside her head, within her heart, and she didn't want to let him go.

Epilogue

Two months later

Daisy stared across the clubhouse at his wife as she danced with her father. For two months Maria had been planning their wedding, and with it being winter, everywhere covered in snow, there hadn't been a place suitable for them to get married.

He'd offered to take her to Vegas, but she wouldn't have any of it. Maria wanted to be married around their friends, and the club. He'd not fought her, and when Duke had offered the use of the club, Maria had squealed. He'd never seen his club Prez looking so terrified as they let all of the old ladies loose.

"She looks happy," Knuckles said, standing beside him.

"Of course she is. She's married to me." Daisy took a sip of his scotch, and kept his gaze on his wife. Beth was stood at the edge of the dance-floor, looking like she wanted to dance, and yet ready to scarper. "Go and ask my sister to dance."

"Excuse me?"

"I know you want to ask her to dance, so do it. She allows you to get close to her. I want her to have a lot of fun, and she enjoys your company." He watched as Knuckles made his way straight toward Beth.

He tensed up as Beth smiled at Knuckles, and then the two were on the dance floor.

It was time for him to get his own wife. Walking across the dance-floor, he grabbed Maria's father's shoulder, and got his attention.

"It's time for me to dance with my wife," he said.

"You'll take good care of her, right?"

"With all of my heart. She's going to be protected and loved."

Her father nodded, slapping his shoulder, and handing Maria back to him.

"Hello, wifey."

"Wifey?"

"Yes, you're mine." He stroked his thumb across her waist. "Did you enjoy today?"

"I did. This has been a dream come true." She rested her head against his chest. "Daisy?"

"Yeah, baby."

"I've got something to tell you."

He kissed the top of her head, closing his eyes as he enjoyed the peace of having her in his arms. It didn't matter what life threw at him, providing he had Maria, his woman, his very reason for living, in his arms.

Daisy couldn't believe he'd lived so long without her. He couldn't imagine sleeping alone. The best part of his day was waking with her in his arms, and falling asleep with her wrapped around him.

"What have you got to tell me?"

"You know how we've been, er, enjoying each other?"

"Yes. I enjoyed this morning before you had to leave me to get ready to marry me." He'd taken her even though Maria had told him he shouldn't. The moment he'd been inside her, she hadn't told him to stop. "I can't wait until I can take you to my room, and fuck your sweet pussy."

"Have you noticed I've not had any wine today?"

"Yeah, I did notice that."

"I've been feeling a little sick in the morning."

"Babe, what's wrong?"

His heart started to pound as he thought of the numerous problems that could be wrong with her. She needed to go to the hospital right now.

"I'm pregnant, Daisy. I took the test this morning after you left me. We're going to have a baby."

Everything seemed to stop, and Maria lifted her head to look at him. He stared into her blue eyes as her words finally took recognition inside his head.

"We're going to have a baby?"

He wasn't quiet, and the whole room stopped to turn toward them.

Maria's cheeks heated, and she nodded.

Looking toward his club brothers, he screamed the news for them to hear, and then pulled the love of his life into his arms. He stroked his fingers across her stomach, knowing he would be the best damn husband and father ever.

The End

www.samcrescent.wordpress.com

SAM CRESCENT

EVERNIGHT PUBLISHING ®

www.evernightpublishing.com

CPSIA information can be obtained
at www.ICGtesting.com
Printed in the USA
BVOW04s1749040617

486014BV00001B/5/P